MW00934167

VISIONS
OF
JUSTICE

Mike Holst

iUniverse LLC
Bloomington

VISIONS OF JUSTICE

Copyright © 2014 Mike Holst.

All rights reserved. No part of this book may be used or reproduced by any means,
graphic, electronic, or mechanical, including photocopying, recording, taping or by
any information storage retrieval system without the written permission of the publisher
except in the case of brief quotations embodied in critical articles and reviews.

This is a work of fiction. All of the characters, names, incidents,
organizations, and dialogue in this novel are either the products
of the author's imagination or are used fictitiously.

iUniverse books may be ordered through booksellers or by contacting:

iUniverse LLC
1663 Liberty Drive
Bloomington, IN 47403
www.iuniverse.com
1-800-Authors (1-800-288-4677)

Because of the dynamic nature of the Internet, any web addresses or links contained in
this book may have changed since publication and may no longer be valid. The views
expressed in this work are solely those of the author and do not necessarily reflect the
views of the publisher, and the publisher hereby disclaims any responsibility for them.

Any people depicted in stock imagery provided by Thinkstock are models,
and such images are being used for illustrative purposes only.
Certain stock imagery © Thinkstock.

ISBN: 978-1-4917-3783-5 (sc)
ISBN: 978-1-4917-3784-2 (e)

Printed in the United States of America.

iUniverse rev. date: 06/18/2014

ALSO BY MIKE HOLST

An Absence of Conscience

The Last Trip Down the Mountain

No Clues in the Ashes

Back To the Ashes

Justice For Adam

Nothing To Lose

A Long Way Back

Coming Home At Last

The Magic Book

ACKNOWLEDGMENTS

My heartfelt thanks to my good friend, wordsmith and editor, Glenda Berndt, for her tireless efforts on this book.

To my special friend Pat McCormick who helped me to get it right.

To all of my readers, wherever you may be, for your encouragement. It's your words of support and praise that inspire all writers to write more.

To my beloved Kitty. May you rest in peace.

PROLOGUE

He saw them coming long before they ever reached the farm. The dust cloud that was being raised, by the vehicle wheels from the speeding convoy, formed contrails of airborne dirt that drifted high above the ripening cornfields into the hot August sky. No one came this far down the dead-end road unless they were coming here. He wasn't expecting company, and neither was Jesse. He had lived with the fear of this day for a long time. They had arrested him once but they wouldn't catch him again. Not this time, anyway. Slowly, and methodically, he backed up several rows deep into the head-high cornfield and squatted down. There were five marked squad cars, and a black panel truck with S.W.A.T. stenciled across the back, in the police convoy. Dogs could be heard barking from the back seat of one of the cars, and the other squads were full of stern-faced men staring straight ahead, their minds on one thing, the mission-at-hand. One car drove crazily across the lush green lawn, careening around the house out of Barry's line of sight, ripping up sod and smashing a trellis covered with purple morning glories, tipping over the birdbath on the way. The resident farm dog cowered on the porch, not sure what to make of it. Car doors opened, and heavily armed men in black vests and Ak5's spilled out, slamming the doors behind them. They had found him, yes, but not for long. He'd been expecting them.

Barry melted deeper into the cornfield, walking fast but not running, and being careful not to disturb or move the stalks. He had already planned this route, and it would take a while before they discovered there was no one home but Jesse. The police dogs would find his trail and that was what worried him the most. However, he had walked this field every day just to stink it up and the dogs wouldn't know which way he went, but they might get lucky. There were loud voices coming from the area of the buildings. They had awakened Jesse by now and were grilling him. He felt bad for the old man who had hired him to tend his crops. He didn't deserve this kind of treatment, but now he was guilty by association—like it or not —because he had harbored a fugitive.

Jesse had suffered a stroke this spring, right after he put the crops in. He had placed a "Farmhand Wanted" in the Help Wanted section of the newspaper, and Barry had answered the ad. It seemed like an attractive option at the time. He had spent his summers, as a teenager, on his uncle's farm in Southern Minnesota, and knew his way around the equipment. This was an out of the way place, fifty miles from the city he had fled from. Right now, he had no idea how they'd found him this time. Barry remembered the words of the Minneapolis Police Chief when he'd told the reporters on television, "We will chase him to the ends of the earth if we have to—he will pay for this."

His breathing was becoming labored, and he could feel the sweat running down his back. He was getting closer to the river, and it wasn't far now, but the sweat was getting in his eyes, making it difficult to see. He wiped his face on his shirtsleeve. His hands were bleeding from hundreds of tiny cuts he had gotten from the dry sharp corn leaves. Then he was at the riverbank and he slipped into the cool water, and swimming diagonally with the current, crossed the water to the opposite shore. The duck boat was just a few feet away. Then he heard the helicopter circling the cornfield.

If he got in the boat now he would be a sitting duck. The river wasn't very wide but it had very little canopy from the trees. He crawled under the boat hoping that, from the air, it would look like a rocky outcropping. The dogs came closer and closer to the river, and the impulse to just take off running across the fields behind him was strong, but deep down, he knew that was suicide. Then, just like that, the sound of the dogs barking was fading farther and farther away. *He would stay put until dark,* he thought, *but no—that would give them more time to bring reinforcements.* He launched the boat; at least the stream and its swift current flowed quickly away from the property.

CHAPTER ONE

It had been a long and difficult journey, that August day from that Minnesota cornfield to the primitive forests of Alaska; and an even more dangerous trip to where he was now. On his flight from the law he had crossed the border into Canada, and then hitched rides on freight trains until he was safely in Alaska. That was four lonely years ago.

But solitary living has a way of driving a man crazy, and he needed to get out of here before he snapped. He had read, "Into the Wild," by Jon Krakauer, which told the story of a young man in a similar situation as the one he was in. It had sent shivers up his spine as he recalled the fate of that man. He had also nearly died of starvation that first winter in the wilderness. Only sharing a moose kill with wolves had saved him. They didn't give the kill up easily, and he had to shoot three of them before they would leave. Those wolves were the only ones who knew where he was. At night he could hear them howling in the woods behind the cabin and he knew that, someday, they wanted to even the score with him. The trapper's cabin was the only piece of luck he'd had. He always lived with the fear the trapper would return and he'd have to leave, but he never did. Finding it on the second week of hiking down this stream had been a Godsend, and it had undoubtedly saved his life. It had been only weeks before winter's fury had arrived with a vengeance.

The trapper's old log cabin had been built so close to the river's bank that you could almost always hear the sound of the rushing water right through the log walls, and you could faintly smell it. That river water outside the door seemed to be a relentless current. It was flowing so fast that it rarely froze as it found its way around the rocks and deadfall that tried to impede its flow on a relentless trip that would take it, eventually, to the sea.

That route was the way of the Chena River, which emptied into the Tanana, and then into the Yukon River. If something got in the current's way, it quickly found its way around it, or was simply swallowed up and taken along with it. The Middle Fork, where he was now, was not a big river by Alaska standards, at least not most of the year, but in the spring it grew wide and deep from the melting snow and ice runoff coming from the White Mountains, where it originated. Many times a year it would leave its banks and creep very close to the cabin door. So far, in the four years he had been here, it had just teased him but the realization that came from the water stains on the log walls told him, shortly after he had found the shelter, that the potential was there to wash him and the cabin away some day. He tried not to think about it, but it was always in the back of his mind, and he hoped he would be gone before that happened.

When the wind was from the east, you could actually smell the fine, sweet, but sultry mist of the river in the air. The river, for anyone living in this wilderness, was as essential to their well-being as his own lifeblood was to his body's existence in this harsh, but pristine country. It had also been his way into the forest maze and it would be his way out someday, and that time was going to be soon.

In the past four years, most of his days were spent just providing for himself, but that was okay because his past, before this time, only haunted him and he had less time to think about it. It was the same past he had come here to escape. It had been hard enough to escape the people who were hunting him; he didn't need to punish himself every day he was here by dredging up what had happened. All he knew for sure was, it wasn't over. Not because he couldn't forget about it—he could and he had—until that nosy detective, after all of those years, had dredged it back up again. He had been exonerated once, but they were convinced he had killed her and they weren't going to stop until they had him locked up for good. He had started a new life after the killing, his first trial and subsequent acquittal. Barry screwed his head on right and became a sober man but then it all came crashing down on him that August day four years ago and now—well, if they wanted a fight, he would give them one. He was tired of hiding, tired of living on the edge of death, tired of being accused of something he hadn't done, and he wasn't going to stand for it any longer. He wasn't guilty, but he was being forced to live as if he was.

He remembered the day the swat team had rushed his house and arrested him for the second time. He knew something was up, but wasn't sure what. There had been rumors around that the case was being reopened. For almost ten years he had lived in peace in that small house in Golden Valley, a western suburb of Minneapolis. He had joined the Lions Club, worked at civic events, and had made a lot of friends. He took the boys to ball games at the Metrodome and the Target Center. The boys, Jessie and Kevin, were Lisa's by a previous marriage but he was the best dad they had ever had. They loved him and he loved them. He didn't love Lisa the same way he had loved Kim, but they had a good life together. Maybe if Kim had lived he would have had kids of his own. That was the plan before she was brutally murdered. But for now he was a free man, and that meant a lot to him.

Lisa had gotten him out on bail again during the second trial, but he had betrayed the law and her, and he had been on the lam ever since. He was found guilty in absentia. Then that day came along at the farm where he had hidden, and he ran farther than he'd ever run before—to this frozen treacherous wilderness. He would go back to Minneapolis when he found the man who killed Kim, and not before. An impossible task way up here in the wilderness, but it was one of the reasons he was leaving. He dreamt about that fateful night a lot up here in the land of the midnight sun, and although it upset him to dream about it, the pieces of the puzzle relating to Kim's murder were forming in his head. It was very vague, yes, but it was something to work with.

Last night, Barry had dug out a festering tooth in the back of his mouth, with his hunting knife, and right now he was out of his mind with pain. The yellow decayed tooth lay in pieces in the bottom of a dirty whiskey glass, beside the cot on a wooden crate. He had drunk half the bottle to get the courage to do it, and the other half afterwards to kill the pain. He had saved his last bottle for just such an occasion. The empty bottle now lay smashed in front of the rock fireplace where he'd thrown it in a pain-filled rage. If it had been the old west he would have poured the whiskey in the wound and today he would be all cured. But it wasn't the old west, and he was out of whiskey, and it still hurt. He was out of a lot of other things right now, including patience. He was out of food and coffee. His ammunition for hunting was running low, but the thing that bothered him the most was, he was out of his mind with thoughts of revenge for the man who had killed Kim, and now he was intent on finding out who it might be. If the cops couldn't find the killer, he would. But that would have to wait for a while, as sweet as the thought might be.

More than once, the night of the murder had appeared to him in a dream. A dream that gave him some hints, but not all of the pieces. All the same, though, it was a dream that had him convinced of his innocence—innocence that he had never doubted. He wished he could just go to sleep and dream the whole story from beginning to end but, so far, that hadn't happened.

He craved a lot of things he used to have, in the life that he had left behind, when he had been on easy street. He was tired of lying low and tired of the punishing life in this cruel wilderness. There is an old adage that says, "Today is the first day of the rest of your life." He had suffered long enough; it was time to make someone else suffer, and that was the man who had killed Kim and gotten away with it. Then, just for spite, maybe the man who had unjustly convicted him of it and who was still hunting him.

He sat on the edge of the bed and ran his hands through his greasy unkempt hair. His undershirt was more gray than white, and was full of holes; both of his last pairs of socks had holes in them, too. Pulling on his worn boots, he stood unsteadily in the middle of the room, looking around. It was a simple, one-room log cabin with a dirt floor. It had served him well for four years and it had kept him alive, but no one deserved to live in this squalor. He walked to the door, took his coat off the hook, and grabbed his rifle off the tabletop. That table and the hardwood slab bed, with two filthy blankets on it, were the only pieces of furniture he'd ever had here. There was a long trek ahead of him; it was the first of October and the long Alaskan winter wasn't far off, and he'd better get started. Slowly, and in pain, he grabbed his pack with all of his belongings and shouldered it. Daylight was scarce in this part of the world. Barry stood in the doorway, looking around the bare bones room. It had never really been a home—more of a hideout than anything. Four long winters had made him weary of its bare log walls. He knew every knot in every log, and every nail that showed through the roof boards. There was nothing here worth keeping any longer, including the few memories he had made. He turned and walked away, his rifle slung over his shoulder, leaving the door open—the way he had found it four years ago.

CHAPTER TWO

In 2007, when Torch Brennan retired from the Minneapolis Homicide Unit, he took almost thirty years of police experience with him. His desire for solving crimes was proving to be a faucet that was hard to shut off at the height of his career, but towards the end, it had stifled to a trickle. That was all right because he had no regrets, he had solved many crimes and been a good and faithful servant of the Minneapolis Police Department. Now he looked forward to nothing more than a life of leisure, time at the cabin in the summer and coffee with his friends in the winter. He had it all figured out and it all sounded very inviting.

His wife, Charlie, was still the County Attorney, and she bent Torch's ear often, discussing cases that came before her. Often enough to peak his interest from time to time, and make him wonder if retiring had been the right thing. True, he was getting old, but there was a big difference between an aging body and an aging mind. One gave you signals of pain that said, "You shouldn't do that anymore," but the other brought wisdom, sensibility and shortcuts to solutions because you knew what worked, and didn't work, because you had been there so many times before.

Today was a perfect October day and he walked slowly around Lake Harriet. The sun was hot in the daylight, but it was chilly in the shade, and he carried his jacket in his hand. He could hear the joggers coming up behind him and stepped to the side to let them pass, hearing their labored breathing and an occasional "Hi" or "On the left" from a few of them. He had never been a runner as a younger man, but he had been a weight lifter, and for many years he took pride in keeping in shape; always going to the gym after work to work out. He had been blessed with a strong body as a young rookie cop. He remembered the times when he walked the beat on Hennepin Avenue, and had twisted many arms behind their backs, and brought thugs to their knees. Yeah, you didn't screw with Torch. He smiled at the thought. *My how times change*, he thought, and kicked at a rock lying on the pathway. *Was that all he was good for now? Kicking rocks?*

He crossed the street and went up the front steps of the old Cape Cod he and Charlie had bought shortly after he retired. She should be home soon as it was Friday, and they had made plans to go up north for one last weekend before they put the boat away and pulled the dock out of the water. *Yeah*, he thought, *getting old wasn't for wimps*. Torch bent over and picked up the mail that had been slipped through the door slot. Nothing much of interest came anymore, and today was no exception, just advertisements and the gas bill. He laid them on the dining room table for Charlie to take care of.

Retirement from the fast-paced life he had lived for so many years as a Minneapolis Detective had left Torch frustrated and bored. He had no real hobbies and he found out fast that his friends, who were still working, had little time for socializing. When he'd left, he had broken the common thread that held them all together for such a long time, and he was on the outside looking in. He heard the crunch of tires on the driveway and looked up to see Charlie pulling in. *Good*, he thought, *sitting around here was driving him nuts*.

She looked so good in her striped pants suit and grey blouse. There were days when he still couldn't believe she had fallen for him. She had much more to offer to their marriage than he had. The door slammed behind her as she walked over and kissed him softly. "Give me a few minutes to change, Babe, and we can hit the road," she said, heading for the stairway and up to the bedroom.

"How was the traffic?" Torch asked, yelling up the stairwell.

"It sucks Torch…like every Friday afternoon. Hey, ask me about Ray when we get on the road. I heard something that might interest you." With that, the bedroom door closed. Torch picked up the food boxes he had packed and took them out to the car.

Charlie had changed into blue jeans and a long-sleeved polo shirt. It would be nippy up north. She brought down two bags and dropped them on the floor. "That's it, my love. I'm ready to go." She gave him such a big mischievous and infectious smile that it made Torch chuckle. He never knew what she was up to next.

They made their way out to 494 and then turned northwest, heading for the outskirts of the city. Charlie lay back in her seat with a soft smile on her face. It would be good to get away. The trip north would take about three hours. Gradually, the buildings thinned out and changed from strip malls and small businesses, to suburban neighborhoods with earth-tone painted homes and an occasional school or park, and then again to small farms and a quiet countryside. Her job, as the County Attorney, gave her little time to get away and she relished these opportunities. It wasn't just all the work and crime she dealt with—this was also an election year and she was in the last two months of the race. Not that she had a serious challenger, but life had taught her to take every threat seriously.

"Hey, you asked me to mention Ray. What's up?" Torch asked, without looking at her.

Charlie sat up and turned slightly in the seat. "Well, he came over to my office this morning. We had a couple of cases coming up that he needed to go over with me, and he asked about you. Then he said something interesting. Seems they got a hit on some DNA test—that goes back about twenty years—to the old Barry Winston case."

Torch turned to look at her briefly. "Wow, I almost forgot about that guy. Whatever happened to him?"

"Guess he's still out there someplace," Charlie said. "But anyway, it seems there was some DNA from that scene where his wife, Kim, was murdered that wasn't Barry's and was never identified, and now they have a match. A guy by the name of Skip something or other…I forget. I know you worked long and hard on that case so I thought it would interest you."

Torch ran his hand through his hair and gave Charlie a serious look. "There is no doubt in my mind, Charlie, that Barry killed his wife. He had more of her blood on him than she did. My only regret is that the son of a bitch skipped bail and we haven't heard from him since. Did Ray say what the DNA was?"

"No, I didn't ask, either. You should stop down and see the guys someday. They all miss you."

Torch didn't answer her. His hands had a tight grip on the steering wheel and his mind was someplace else. Ray Edmonds and Torch hadn't worked together that much—not until the last few years before he retired. They had a few lunches together, and Torch had helped him with the transition from Detective to Chief of Detectives. You had to learn how to kiss ass and be a politician—something Torch was never that good at so he wasn't much of a teacher. Maybe he would stop over next week and see Ray.

"Let's stop in St. Cloud for lunch," Charlie said, reclining once more without opening her eyes, "Besides, you owe me one."

"Oh, my God," Torch laughed. "The Hennepin County Attorney making the big bucks and she screws her poor old retired husband out of lunch."

"Keep it up, buddy, and you'll get screwed out of more than that." She sat up and playfully punched him in the shoulder.

Torch jerked the steering wheel and said, "Hey, you almost made me go in the ditch."

St. Cloud was almost at the halfway mark on the trip and they stopped there often, for food and bathroom breaks, when they went up north.

"Where we going?" Torch asked.

"Your choice, babe, but it better be I-Hop." Then she giggled... that same "little girl giggle" that always melted Torch's heart.

With full stomachs and empty bladders they hit the road again. Charlie reclined in her seat once more, closing her eyes, and was soon snoozing.

Torch stared at the road ahead, with the fields and woods around him, but his mind was back in the cities, in a blood-splattered bedroom, twenty years ago. He could still smell the copper odor of all the blood and carnage. He could still see the dead body of Kim Winston spread-eagled on the bed—her blood-soaked pajamas stuck to her body, her vacant eyes staring at the ceiling.

In the kitchen sat her husband, Barry, splattered with his wife's blood, and drunk out of his mind trying, through his sobs, to explain what had happened, but the detectives would have none of his story. It was too obvious what had happened.

The knife that had carved Kim up was still lying on the bed, with Barry's bloody fingerprints all over it. "Yes, it was their knife," he admitted, "from the butcher block in the kitchen." But he hadn't used it on her. He had been drunk, he reasoned with the police, and passed out, and when he woke up it was all over. The crime scene specialist had come and processed the scene and except for one wayward sample, all they could find was Barry and Kim's DNA. That one sample, that was not a match for Barry or Kim, was a hair found in Kim's hand. It was explained away at the trial by the prosecuting attorney, as a wayward hair brought home from work by Kim, who was a hairdresser. Barry Winston was found guilty of second-degree murder, but he was let out on bail and hadn't shown up for sentencing. He had been on the lam ever since.

It was one piece of unfinished business in Torch's long career that still bothered him.

Barry stood on the riverbank looking for fish. He had walked all day and he was tired and hungry. The river was shallow here—littered with rocks and boulders. He could shoot a fish if he saw one, or he could try to spear them with his knife. He preferred the spearing, because he didn't have much ammunition left, and marauding bears and wolves could use up a lot of it in a hurry.

It had been so long since he came here that he didn't recognize much of the terrain. All he knew was the river brought him in and the river would take him out. The elevation was higher here and he could feel the cold wind blowing down the river. Winter wasn't that far off.

Finally, he spotted a sucker floating lazily next to a rock. He found a dead branch, and using his bootlace, he lashed his knife to it and waited. Slowly, he brought the homemade spear over the fish and then lunged. The water boiled and stirred up sediment, but he knew he had his fish by the violent action on the end of the stick. If he just picked it up he risked the fish sliding off, so he held it to the bottom until he could see what he had. Then he retrieved it.

Barry built a fire, dried out his shoes and socks, and cooked his fish. He had found a place under a boulder where there was some shelter out of the wind. He spread out his sleeping bag and crawled in it just as the sun was setting over the treetops. His rifle was cocked, loaded and within reach. Like the fish, he might be some critter's meal if he wasn't careful.

Tonight, as with every night before he dozed off, he let the hatred in his heart for his wife's killer, and Torch Brennan, fester some more. It had been a long time of suffering and wondering what tomorrow would bring. It was time to make it all go away. It was time for payback. That thought never left his mind for a minute.

CHAPTER THREE

Charlie and Torch had kicked back that weekend, forgetting about what was going on in the city, and had spent a relaxing two days. They had gotten in some fishing, and were also able to get some work done around the place. There was always something that needed fixing, but it was a labor of love, at least for Torch. On Saturday evening they went for a long walk in the woods and then, that evening, laid by the fireplace in the twilight hours, remembering that magical weekend so long ago when they had made love right there. They preferred the bedroom now, but all too soon, the weekend was over before any lovemaking could take place. Torch packed the car back up and went through his mental checklist once more. All the doors and windows locked and the fire out in the fireplace. The garbage bag was in his hand as he made one last walk though the cabin. They would need to come up once more, to take the dock out of the lake and put the old boat away for winter.

They had made a big decision this weekend. They were going to tear the old cabin down and have a new house built. Something more comfortable, and maybe a place they would spend a lot more time at as their lives wound down. Charlie was having thoughts about four more years in the County Attorney's office and then she would retire, too. The politics were eating her up.

Torch seemed to be more preoccupied than usual over the weekend. He had always been a thinker, and right after he'd retired that part of him seemed to have gone away, but now it was back. Charlie wondered what was on his mind but was afraid to ask. Maybe it was the decision with the cabin. It had been in his family a long time. Changes come hard to aging people but, as much as she loved the lake and the country, she was tired of roughing it, and anyway, they needed something to spend their money on.

"Ready to hit the road?" she said, coming out of the outhouse.

"Yeah, let's try and beat some of the traffic," mumbled Torch. It was always a downer to leave.

There was little to talk about on the way home and Charlie was soon dozing again. The rhythmic sound of the tires on the road had a way of lulling her to sleep, and the previous night had been short.

But as for Torch, his thoughts went back to the Barry Winston case that, somehow, his mind would not let him forget. Not now, anyway. Charlie had lit the fire again and she wasn't even involved with it, but she had brought it up. Tomorrow he would go see Ray. He had to put this to rest. It was the one unfinished piece of business that still bothered him. Barry was getting away with murder and that didn't sit well with Torch. For a long time he thought Barry, and his escape, would just go away when he retired and it could become someone else's cross to bear. Seemed it wasn't so.

Sometime during the long Alaskan night, clouds had floated across the face of the full moon—ominous clouds, filled with moisture and electricity. Two things that came from it, thunder and raindrops, awakened Barry. The rock he was partway under would give him some shelter, but he was also in a depression that would fill up with water. He searched in his backpack for some plastic and covered himself as best he could in the darkness, making an apron to drain the water away from him. The falling rain soon extinguished his campfire and now it was really dark and something else was bothering him. Something was in his sleeping bag with him.

It was small and scurrying around in the bottom of his sleeping bag. Must be a mouse or a shrew, he reasoned. Either way, he wasn't going to unzip the bag again; it could just stay there.

Barry awoke to sunshine staring him in the face, and the rodent that had eluded him last night, sleeping in the middle of his chest. If he tipped his head up as far as he could, the small mouse came into view. His fist impulse was to grab it, crush it and throw it as far as he could. But then, as he watched its tiny belly going in and out with its respirations he had a sense that, for the first time in a long time, he wasn't alone. Slowly, he brought his hand up and cradled it in his palm. It showed no fear and its tiny whiskers tickled his hand. He sat up and put it in his lap, but it still stayed put. He found a few shards of fish left from last night and put them in front of its nose, and it hungrily ate them down.

Barry had rolled up his bag and belongings, and put them on top of the rock he had slept under. He relieved himself on the fire ashes, and drank some water. It was time to hit the trail; he still had a ways to go. There, sitting by his foot, the little mouse still sat. He reached down and it crawled into his hand. For a second, Barry looked at it and then, smiling, he put it in his pocket. For once, he had a traveling companion.

He wasn't sure how far it was to the tiny outpost of Kapitsa, which sat in the fork of two rivers. He only knew that, when he came here, it had been a four-day walk to the cabin he had found and lived in for the last four miserable years. Had he overreacted in his flight from justice, running away to this desolate place? Maybe, but then for several years before he had thought that he was safe. Then they found him and came for him again. Now, he was just sick of the whole miserable game. There was only one way to stop it and that was to stop the man who would not give up looking for him, and more importantly, find the person who had killed Kim. This detective… this Torch Brennan…had made his life a living hell, and it was time put an end to it.

It was a good day for walking. The temperature was in the fifties and the skies were clear. For the most part, the hiking was easy because it was high ground, and the brush and swamps were few. Around noon he shot a rabbit, and cleaned it, and put it in his pack. He had very little ammunition left, but the rabbit would be his supper. His and that sneaky little mouse that was still in his pocket. That was a good name for the mouse, and he made up his mind to keep him for a while. "Sneaky" it would be.

Just before dark he found a gully that would keep him out of the wind. The clouds had floated in and out of the blue sky all day—never forming into anything formidable, but tonight, the sultry smell of wet weather was in the air. It was that heavy kind of air that comes in as the precursor to some kind of moisture, and tonight it might be cold enough for it to turn to snow. In Alaska, once the ground was covered, it seldom warmed up again until spring.

The gully had, in its bottom, a small stream that eventually emptied into the river. A stream so small that it seemed inconsequential to the volume of water the river carried. However, unlike the river that muddied its waters with its turbulence, this diminutive stream ran cool and clear. Most likely it was a spring that had bubbled up from some far away rock formation in the distant foothills. Barry drank his fill, and then washed up as much as he could without getting too chilled. He also filled his canteen, made a fire and found shelter under a large spreading spruce tree.

As he sat down to wait for his rabbit to finish cooking over the fire he had built, he extracted the mouse from his pocket; and holding it in his hand, he stroked its fine gray fur. Its eyes glistened, and its whiskers twitched, and it seemed to enjoy the attention it was getting. As for Barry—he enjoyed giving the attention. To an outsider it would seem inconceivable that this man, whose heart had been so hardened with hate and revenge for the people who had wronged him, could find it in his heart to give such loving attention to this little creature.

Ray Edmonds had been head of the homicide division ever since Torch had retired. He had come into it full of energy, and a lot of ideas or, as Torch called it, piss and vinegar. But he, too, gradually got into a rut with new murders and investigations coming almost every week. It was a shuffle game in homicide, pulling detectives from one case to another, and seemingly, never catching up. For Ray, he had enjoyed the hunt when he was a detective, but now was caught up in a paper blizzard and never-ending budget and personnel problems. Some days he yearned to go back to what he was doing before he took the job. He had little time to socialize with the men and women who worked for him and who were, at one time, his close friends. Being boss had closed that door.

Torch called Ray on Monday morning. He had to get to the bottom of this. It had bothered him for two days now, and had ruined his weekend up north. For most good detectives, a case is closed when the perpetrator is caught, tried and convicted. Barry Winston met all of those benchmarks, but had never served one day in prison. The fact that he was free all of these years was troubling, but Torch had always reasoned he had done his job. Now though, that was proving to not be the case. The case had long ago gone to the cold case files. Now this DNA thing had come up and he had to get to the bottom of it. As far as he knew, he had never wrongfully convicted anyone. Well, to be truthful, he had never convicted anyone, anyway—that was for the courts to do. But he could damn well make the case for someone's conviction, and he had, many times.

They were back at Whitey's for lunch. This old restaurant had long been the haunt of the old cops on the Minneapolis P.D. Now, as the Department was getting older and the cops were getting younger, it was falling out of favor with most of them. They loved the fast food places and the food trucks.

Torch's farewell party had been held here at Whitey's, and that was the last time either of them had been there. Actually, Ray didn't want to be here today, either, but Torch was buying so what the hell.

The bells above the door tinkled as they went in, just as they always had.

"Jeez, Torch, just one whiff and I got the shits already," Ray quipped, making a sour face. "It took two years for my digestive system to get back to normal and now here we go again. If you order that damn meatloaf I'm going to puke on top of it."

"What did you have for breakfast?" Torch asked. "Hope it's something that goes with my meatloaf, if I have to eat it again for you."

They slid into one of the red vinyl booths that were showing their age with small rips and tears.

"I hear this place is on one of the super funds clean-up sites," Ray said, smiling.

"Hi, Torch. Long time no see." The cheery greeting came from Wendy, who had always been Torch's favorite waitress for at least twenty years. Those same years had not been good to Wendy and she now had more than a few more pounds to stuff into her tight waitress outfit, and it looked like her boobs were going to fly out and smack someone in the face. She had dyed her hair platinum blond, and today she had a bright red ribbon holding back a long ponytail that most horses would have died for.

"Missed you, baby," Torch said, patting her arm. "We would both like a generous helping of Whitey's meatloaf."

"Hey, bring me a barf bag, too, if you would," Ray said, smiling.

"Two meatloaf and one barf bag. Is that it?" Torch nodded his head.

"No barf bag for me. I got to eat Ray's breakfast over again, too, and I'm on a diet."

Wendy smiled, not knowing what he meant by that, but she could well imagine. She'd been dealing with cops for twenty years here at Whitey's, and had heard all of their comments and harassment a thousand times, and loved every moment of it.

"So, what's on your mind, Torch? You don't buy anyone lunch without a reason." Ray was wolfing down his lunch, and talking with his mouth full of food.

"Well, Charlie said you had something new on the Barry Winston case, and I wondered what was going on. Do you have any idea where he is?"

Ray stopped eating and wiped his mouth on a napkin. "Yeah. Yeah, we do have something. We got a match from a guy named Skip Hendricks, who was just accused of killing someone in South Carolina. They took his DNA, and it matched some hair found at the scene of your case way back then."

"Going to do anything with it?" Torch asked.

Ray shrugged his shoulders. "Not unless something changes. We're too damn busy to screw around with cold cases, and by the way, I don't know where he is or I might be tempted."

"So why tell me?"

Ray looked at Torch out of the top of his eyes, his head lowered, as he mopped up the gravy on his plate with a slice of bread. "I thought maybe you'd want to take it on."

"You forget—I'm retired."

"I know. But I also know you have more than a passing interest in this case. Look, I have some money in an account we use to pay private dicks that help us out. Keep track of your time and I'll get you reimbursed. But not at that lofty salary you were making when you quit."

"Retired," Torch corrected him.

"Yeah, well, whatever you call it, are you in or out?"

Torch was drumming his fingers on the tabletop, thinking. *He had nothing better to do, and maybe this would clear up some things for him as far as this case was concerned. Then again, he had no idea where Barry was so maybe it would accomplish nothing. Hell, he might as well, what did he have to lose?*

"Alright, I'm in."

"Good," Ray said. "Stop by the office and I'll give you the file. Now, if you will pardon me, I want to leave before I shit my pants. Jeez, Torch, don't bring me here again. My guts are rolling." With that, Ray got up and left. He looked over his shoulder to see if Torch was watching him, and made a big production out of lifting his leg and shaking his pant leg.

Torch laughed, and put down a twenty. Wendy was nowhere around. He would have liked to say goodbye. He stepped out on Marquette into the brisk October air. Turning up his collar, he walked back in a stiff north breeze to the parking ramp. He'd come down tomorrow and get that file.

CHAPTER FOUR

Barry turned his collar up, and pulled his head in for protection from the wind, as he picked his path up the steep side of a rocky ridge, covered with towering pine trees. If you were on vacation the scenery here was breathtaking, but when you were just trying to survive, it wasn't so memorable. From the memory of his walk into this place four years ago, he was getting close to the Native American settlement now, and although he wouldn't get there today, he would be there sometime tomorrow. One more night in the wild with Sneaky, the mouse, sleeping on his chest—just like he did last night. They had eaten more fish last night as he didn't want to waste any more of the few rifle rounds he had left. He had found a large northern pike in the shallows, still living but incapacitated, with a sucker fish half its size stuck in its throat. If he had learned one thing living in the wild—there was plenty to eat if you knew where to look. Even in the winter.

A pack of wolves had been following him today, but had kept their distance. He had caught sight of them on two occasions as he crossed some wide-open spaces. At this time of the year they shouldn't be too hungry. He hoped they wouldn't become a problem tonight, but with any luck he should be out of their territory before then. Most times they were reluctant to get into another wolf pack's domain and he had a feeling, knowing what he knew about wolves, that they were more interested in the territory they were in than anything else. The deer were plentiful this year, and so were the moose calves, so they shouldn't want to bother him. *Not much meat on my ass,* he thought. There were grizzly bears around, however, and they were not something to take lightly, although he hadn't seen any so far. Most of them were born pissed off. They only came to the rivers to fish when the spawn was on and that wasn't now.

His plan was to sell his rifle to the natives, or whoever gave him the best price, for passage on one of the many boats or planes to Fairbanks, and for buying some new clothes and boots. After that, he had no real thought-out plan except to get back to the states eventually, find the person who had murdered Kim, and teach Torch Brennan a lesson. If he needed some extra money jobs would be plentiful in Salta, as the settlement was called. A lot of the people who worked there in the summer, during the tourist season, would be leaving now for warmer climates. The area was known for fishing and fly-ins to many of the hundreds of lakes and rivers that dotted the area. Most of the fishermen flew into the tiny settlement on the short gravel airstrip, that paralleled the river, but some of them came up the river by boat.

That night, Barry felt more relaxed. He couldn't see "the light at the end of the tunnel" when it came to getting to Fairbanks, but he could see the tunnel and that gave him hope. Supper was some wild rice he had harvested, and a venison rump roast off a young buck deer that got too curious.

He had put the rice in the same pocket as Sneaky, and when he took his little friend out to give him some air, his little belly was bulging. Barry roared with laughter. It was the first good laugh he had had in a long time. There wasn't a lot of difference between the color of the rice and Sneaky's droppings, but what the hell; it was rice once, wasn't it? They both slept well that night—with full bellies and an unusually warm night.

Tuesday morning, right after Ray got to work, Torch was there to pick up the file, but first, Torch rode out with him to a call by the Lowry Avenue Bridge. Someone had found a dead body on the bank of the river. It could be a homeless person or it could be another drug deal gone badly. The victim's face was literally shot off—most likely by a shotgun blast.

"Jeeze, Ray. All I wanted was that file, and now you got me out here helping you do your job. I saw enough of this shit when I was working."

"Aw, blow it out your ass, Torch. One more dead druggie ain't going to keep you awake tonight."

"Keeping me awake, that's Charlie's job, if you get my drift," Torch muttered, and then wished he hadn't said it, because now his sex life was going to be the subject.

"Oh. Now you're going to tell me you're still on your honeymoon, and you can't get enough of each other. Torch, your wiener retired before you did, and you know it." Ray chuckled at his attempt at humor.

Torch didn't answer him. He was looking at the quiet river as it floated by, and remembering a murder from a long time ago. A young college coed, who had been brutally murdered, her body dumped in the river to spend the better part of the winter season imprisoned under the ice. It had taken over ten years to solve the case, but solve it he did. It was one of the cases he was especially proud of. Like this case with Barry, it wasn't done overnight.

He turned his attention back to the body. The coppery scent of blood was in the air even though the large puddle of gore had congealed, under the man's head, into a mass reminiscent of Danish dessert. He turned and walked away. There was, for Torch, a bad memory on most corners of this city. He just wanted to get that file and go home. He remembered now why he had retired and was having second thoughts about getting involved again. *Well, it was just in an advisory role,* he reasoned.

At last, Ray walked up the hill, and reappeared at the car where Torch was sitting in the front seat, with the door open, looking bored. Opening the trunk, he peeled off his blue rubber gloves and threw them inside. "No watch, no rings and no billfold," he said, coming around to the other side of the car and sliding behind the wheel. "No teeth left so he is going to be hard to identify if his prints aren't on file. But those five hundred dollar boots and that leather coat says this was no homeless man."

"Let's go get that file," Torch said, refusing to comment on the dead man under the bridge."

Charlie had been one of the most progressive county attorneys that Hennepin County had ever seen. For way too long people had gotten away with murder, and too many other things, because there had been a reluctance to aggressively pursue most felons in the courts. Under her direction, she let it be known that she wanted convictions, and not deals cut just to clear the court's dockets.

When Torch was working, there had been a few times that defense attorneys had used his and Charlie's relationship in their defense— claiming the police department and the attorney's office were in some kind of a collusion to find people guilty, and that justice served was often not justice at all, but politically motivated. Not that Charlie needed any help in that department. She was well respected and well admired for the way she ran her department. But when Torch retired, that problem had gone away.

She had no idea, when Ray talked to her the other day, what he wanted to get together with Torch about; she had just relayed the message. Had she known what was going to come out of this, she would probably have kept her mouth shut.

For Barry, the long trek was over and not a day too soon. When he awoke this morning about an inch of snow was on the ground, and despite the fact that it melted before noon, he knew that the worst was yet to come and soon, here in the Yukon. This was no place for a man to be in the winter without a decent shelter.

There was a rare beauty about this unspoiled land and its wild creatures, but after four years, he'd had his fill of it. He had a mission to do now, and then he just wanted to settle down someplace, in peace and obscurity.

The last few miles brought more and more sightings of boats and people along the river. For a lot of the natives, it was their last chance to net fish before the river froze over. The moose hunt was on, too, and he saw several boats laden down with meat and tired hunters.

Over a rise and there it was, at the confluence of the Chena and some tributary he didn't know the name of. Barry was on a rocky ledge, overlooking the frontier town below him, and he felt like a soldier coming home, at last, from the war. In reality, the battle had been won for now, but the war was far from over.

For a while he rested and gathered his thoughts. Then, taking Squeaky out of his pocket and holding him in his hand, he showed him the town below while he talked softly to his little friend. Right now, Squeaky was his only friend. Then, putting him back, he carefully picked his way down the well-worn stony path to the main street of Salta.The general store was nearly empty as Barry walked in. A cluster of bells rang above the door, and an old bespectacled man popped his head up from behind the counter.

"How can I help you?" he said.

"Well, I need to strike a bargain," Barry said. "I need to get to Fairbanks and I need some fresh clothing, boots, coat and a room for the night, and all I have to my name is this rifle."

The old man adjusted his glasses as he peered at the rifle—holding it out at arm's length. "Weatherby," he said, "and a nice one. Tell you what, pick out what you need and then we can talk." Barry left the rifle leaning against the counter. He found some new boots and a warm leather coat, two pair of jeans, two flannel shirts, and some long underwear, topping it off with a bag of wool socks. He dumped them on the counter.

The old man dug through the pile, writing down some numbers on a pad. He clucked his tongue as he gathered his thoughts. "I can get you to Fairbanks tomorrow, put you up for the night, throw in the clothing and boots and give you two hundred dollars."

He had hoped for more, but he was in no position to bargain. Barry nodded his head.

The hot shower was the first one he'd had in four years and it felt so good. He had kept clean in the wild, but always bathing in the ice-cold river or heating water in a pan in the cabin. He cut his hair and shaved, leaving just a short goatee and a mustache. He had bought some supplies at the store, too, and he had also bought a small leather pouch to keep Squeaky in. He didn't want mouse turds in his new jacket pocket or his food anymore, but he wasn't going to abandon his little friend.

Barry lay down on the bed and closed his eyes. Out on the street he could hear four wheelers, and dogs barking. The riverboat left for Fairbanks at seven in the morning. He set the alarm and faded off into a deep sleep. Outside, under the cloud cover, the first real snowfall of the season fell softly to the ground. Barry had a grimace on his face for he was dreaming thoughts that were painful. He was lying beside her as the stranger hacked her body to pieces, but he still couldn't see who he was.

Torch had the entire file out of the box, and spread out all over the dining room table. There were pictures of the murder scene, and Kim's battered and bloody body laying spread-eagled on the bed in her pajamas. The pajama top was pushed up under her chin and one of her breasts, almost severed, hung off to the side. Her eyes were open slits that stared out at you, and you wished they had recorded the last thing they saw, so he could somehow retrieve it. The white bedding bore testament to the savagery of the attack. Her mouth was set in a grimace; the tongue protruding slightly between two rows of perfect white teeth.

Torch turned the photos over. He didn't need them as a reminder—he could still picture it—an indelible memory that still, to this day, haunted him. He wasn't squeamish, and it had nothing to do with the body and death and the gruesome scene. It only had to do with the fact that the man who did this was still on the loose. It was one of the things that had been left unfinished when he retired.

Carefully, he read the coroner's report again, trying hard to come to some other conclusion than the one he came to many years ago, but it wasn't there. Except for this new evidence that had come forth, he would have blown the whole thing off, but in every good investigation you try as hard to exonerate the falsely accused as you do to convict the guilty.

It was just some hairs that had been found in Kim's hand that had brought this whole thing back on. At the trial, they had been explained away by the fact that Kim was a hairdresser by trade, and she brought home hair from other people quite often, but not from a man named Skip. She worked in a women's salon and had never cut men's' hair.

Skip Hendricks was his name and Torch had some roadwork to do. *Where was he the night Kim died?* He looked at the rap sheet. Hendricks would have been in his twenties when this happened. He had been arrested several times over the years for various offenses, but the one that got Torch's attention was an arrest three years ago, in Milwaukee, for sexual assault. It was as good a place as any to start.

Barry was sitting on the dock a whole hour before the riverboat captain showed up and allowed them to board. Barry, and some natives that were obviously still drunk from the night before, were the only ones on board, but they kept to the other end of the boat, and he tried to be as inconspicuous as possible. The last thing he wanted was trouble of any kind. It wasn't a very big boat by riverboat standards, maybe about thirty feet in length. Except for the wheelhouse and boiler area it was open to the elements, but it was covered and that kept the light rain off the crew and passengers. The crew was only one man, who ran the boiler on the aging boat, and the captain, who was a dead ringer for the old Hollywood cowboy Gabby Hayes. Hell, he even sounded like him as he shouted orders to get underway.

The boat had made this trip from Salta to Fairbanks twice a week for years. In the spring when the fish were spawning it was packed, but this was the off-season now. It eased away from the dock and into the current; the trip would only take about a day. Barry reached into his bag and brought out an apple he had packed and sat back to enjoy the scenery of this beautiful land. It looked the same as it had four years ago. This time was different, though. He wasn't running from anyone—this time he was going back to make things right and even the score.

CHAPTER FIVE

"What is all of this?" Charlie asked, "And what is it doing on my dining room table?"

"This is what Ray wanted to talk to me about," Torch answered, looking up at her from the tops of his eyes, as Charlie was standing over him. "It's on the table because it never gets used for anything, anyway, and I needed the space."

Charlie was engrossed in some pictures. "Is this the Barry Winston case?"

"Yes, it is."

"Have they never caught him?"

"No, and now they say they have someone else whose DNA was at the scene."

"Holy crap, Torch! It's like twenty some years since the trial. Why are they digging this up now?" Charlie bent down, and kissed the top of his head. "You smell like cigarette smoke—have you been cheating again?"

Torch didn't answer her question about the smoking, but went on to say, "It's a cold case and Ray got some federal funds to work on this crap, but he doesn't have any people so he asked me if I wanted to. Winter is coming, and I'm bored out of my skull anyway, so I thought…"

Charlie interrupted him. "Are you sure you want to get involved in this, Torch? You retired last year because you couldn't stand the corruption and ass- kissing in the department, and now you're crawling back? You need to think about that."

"I did, and I'm going to do it. This was my case, and I never closed it out, and it bothers me."

"Okay, if that's what you want, but get your shit off of my table."
Charlie walked across the room and headed upstairs to change
clothes. *I love this old fart,* she thought, *but I will never understand
him, and that guy isn't fooling me. He was smoking again.*

Torch picked up all of the papers and pictures and put them back
in the folder. He'd call Ray in the morning. *Maybe this was a big
mistake, dredging up the past again.* He shook his head to clear the
thought.

Barry's feet hurt from the stiff new leather boots but, otherwise,
he was feeling good. The boat had made two other stops at small
settlements and now there were about twenty people on board, most
of them Native Americans going to Fairbanks to party, and then look
for work when their money ran out. It was raining harder now and you
could feel the moisture in the air; it wasn't that far from changing to
snow. Slipping his hand in his pocket and then, inserting his finger in
the little pouch, he could feel the soft fur of Sneaky. The little mouse's
whiskers twitched against his finger as if to say, "All is right in here."

The river level was low and the boat proceeded carefully, trying
to avoid rocks and deadheads. Once they were stuck on a sand bar for
a few minutes, but the captain managed to rock them free and they
were on their way. Right now, they were skirting the riverbank as the
only deep channel seemed to be right next to it. Overhead, branches
from trees scraped along the tin roof of the boat. So far, outside of
some small fishing boats, there had been no other traffic on the river.

Barry had closed his eyes and was meditating. He seemed to be
mellowing as he came closer and closer to society, even though he
didn't realize it. All of those years living alone had turned him into
something even he didn't like. Now he saw people laughing and
having conversations with each other. Sitting directly across from
him was a young man and woman, obviously in love. The man was
trying his best to keep her warm in the cold air, and she was snuggled
tightly under his chin, her dark eyes sparkling in the twilight from
the lone bulb that hung over their heads. They both looked like they
were at peace with the world. *When would he find his peace?*

Barry had slept away most of the day as the boat made its way
to Fairbanks. He hadn't slept well last night, being preoccupied with
the future and what he was going to do and how he was going to do

it. There had been a time in his life when he oozed confidence. He needed to get that mindset back if he was going to be successful.

"Six more miles," the Captain shouted out.

Six more miles and he would be back in civilization, Barry thought. It was scary, but at the same time, he knew it was time to make peace in his life. There were people out there who still wanted to hurt him; who wanted to lock him up for the rest of his life. That wasn't going to happen, as he had made up his mind he would never be taken alive if it came to that. He had no real plans right now, but he felt confident the plans would come to him, and he couldn't lose sight of what he had come back to do.

The riverboat slipped into its mooring, in downtown Fairbanks, and Barry stepped off onto the icy pier. The first order of business would be to find a place for the night. He only had two hundred dollars between him and starvation. Maybe the best place for now would be a mission, if he could find one. A squad car came down the street and Barry waved to him and the cop saluted him back. There was a time when he would have ducked his head, and turned away, but he had learned that was an admission that he was trying to avoid the police. For now, he wanted to fit in.

He'd walked just a few blocks in the slushy snow when he saw a small red sign through the falling flakes that said, "Shelter." Looking up, he saw that it was part of a Catholic Church complex, with a school and a large wooden church. It just might be what he was looking for.

The door to the basement of the church had a small hand-written sign that said, "Bed and breakfast two dollars." Underneath was some smaller hand writing in pencil that said, "No one turned away."

It felt good to be inside. Cautiously, he walked down the wet steps in his slick boots, to another door that opened into the basement. Inside, the lights were dim and several people were sleeping on cots with gray wool blankets pulled over them. Across the room, from behind an old wooden desk, a young man motioned for him to come over.

Barry spoke first, "I need a cot for the night," he said. "I can pay," and he gave the man two dollars. He was handed a blanket and a pillow and pointed in the direction of an empty cot. Then the man said, "God bless and good night."

As he lay there, trying to gather his thoughts, Barry thought back to his childhood in North Minneapolis. His dad left the family when he was thirteen and his mother, who was a staunch Catholic, raised him and his sisters in the faith. Barry had grown up being a server, and going to Catholic grade school. Then, after graduation he had met Kim, who was not Catholic. Gradually, he had left his faith behind him. He looked across the room to the statue of the blessed virgin. For a while he looked at the face on the statue, and it seemed as if she was smiling down at him. *How did the prayer go he had said so often as a child?* "Hail, Mary, full of grace. The Lord is with…" he drifted off to sleep.

When he woke up he could smell bacon cooking, and it reminded him that he hadn't eaten in a day and a half. Someone else hadn't eaten, either, and he put his finger into the pouch in his pocket, and the little mouse responded to his touch with twitching whiskers. It was time to get them both some breakfast. A lot of the people were still sleeping, or at least giving the impression they were. No one wanted to go out in the cold any faster than they had to.

Barry folded up his blanket and took it and the pillow back over to the same old desk where, last night, the young man had given them to him. The desk was unoccupied, but there was a handwritten note that said, "Breakfast in the dining hall" and an arrow drawn on the bottom of the note pointed the way.

There were half a dozen old men sitting at the tables in front of trays of food, all seemingly trying to put some space between them and the others. No one was in a social mood.

"Good morning," she said. "I'm Sister Joanna. Can I get you anything?"

"Just breakfast," Barry smiled.

The sister was old and wrinkled, but her smile was bright and her eyes showed genuine concern for him.

"This is very nice of you," Barry said, taking a tray and sliding it down the counter in front of the steam table.

"Thank God, not us," she said. Just then, the same young man who he had talked to last night came through the door, wearing black and a Roman collar. He was the parish priest. He took a tray and got in line behind Barry.

"Did you sleep well?" he asked.

"I did," Barry answered, "and I want to thank you for your hospitality." The two men took their breakfast and coffee, and sat down beside each other. Barry would have preferred to be alone, but he was the beggar in the priest's house. The young pastor reached across his body and extended his hand. "I'm Father Kevin Perkins," he said. "Are you from around here?"

"No. No I'm not. I just came into town last night. I need to find some work so I can get back home. I don't have much for money."

"Where's home?" Father asked." Were you just looking for shelter last night or…" He stopped in mid-sentence. He was fishing for more information but didn't want to appear nosy.

"Minnesota," Barry said, and then wished he had said someplace else, but lying to a priest wasn't easy. He just wouldn't get any more specific than that, but the young cleric didn't press him for any other information.

"I'm Catholic," Barry said, as he mopped up the last bit of egg yolk with the rest of his biscuit, and then wondered why he had said it.

"Maybe I can help you find work," Father said. He didn't comment on Barry's declaration about being Catholic. "I do have some connections around here, and there are a lot of jobs. What is your line of work?"

Running from the law, he thought to himself. "I was a carpenter," he finally said.

"Well, you're in the right place. So was Jesus," the priest chuckled at his little joke. "Look, I have this parishioner who has a construction company. Come by tomorrow morning for breakfast and I'll have an answer for you—if he needs anyone or not. Seems to me he was hiring as he has some projects to get done before winter. Want some more to eat? There's plenty." The priest looked at his watch and excused himself.

"Thanks, I could use some more." Barry took his tray and went back up to the steam table. This time, he took an extra biscuit and put it in his pocket for his friend.

Father Kevin seemed nice, he thought. *Most of the priests he had known were old and gray. They had sad eyes and always seemed tired and preoccupied. This man was in his late thirties or early forties. He had a full head of blond hair, and blue eyes that seemed to sparkle when he smiled. He appeared to actually be enjoying living out here at the end of the earth. Go figure,* he thought.

Ray and Torch sat in Ray's office. Ray, with his feet up on the desk, and a toothpick making the rounds of his mouth as if it was looking for a place to park itself. "You still have a permit to carry, Torch?"

"Yep. You think I might have to shoot someone?"

"Do you think you could hit a bull in the ass? The guys back here said the only thing you could shoot off was your mouth."

"Want a duel?" Torch pointed his forefinger at Ray, and then pretended to shoot and blow the smoke away.

"Naw, the Chief gets all pissed off when we have duels. Besides, Charlie would get mad if I shot you, and she'd hate me."

"She hates you already." Torch said, and then his face took on a more serious look. "Where do I find this so-called DNA match? I mean the donor, not the sample. This Skip dude or whatever his name is."

"Hendricks. He's in a cell in Milwaukee. I already got you a plane ticket, and you leave tomorrow."

"Pushy bastard, aren't you. The guy's, supposedly, been running away for twenty years and you got me going out of here tomorrow?"

"He gets out of jail the day after tomorrow."

"I thought he was being held on murder charges?"

"Not sure why, but they have to cut him loose. That's all I know."

"Speaking of running away, there has been no recent sighting of Barry Winston, right?"

Ray slipped his feet off the desk and walked over to the window to look at where all the sirens were coming from. The city streets were like a canyon between the big buildings, and the sirens seemed to be coming from everywhere. "Nothing for the last four years, my friend. We had a picture of him on a wanted poster, hanging in the office for a while, but the lieutenant took it down. Said it looked too much like his brother-in–law."

"If you see him, tell him it looked a lot like his wife to me."

"You tell him that. That crabby old bastard would shoot you." Torch was going out the door as Ray was talking. "Eight o'clock flight; your ticket will be at Will Call," Ray shouted at him as he was leaving.

Torch tipped his hat and kept on walking. It was good to be working again.

Skip Hendricks knew he was getting company tomorrow, but he had no idea who. *Didn't care, either.* He was getting out the day after tomorrow, and that was good enough for him. Right now, he was being held on suspicion of murder down in North Carolina, but the witness refused to testify so they were going to have to let him go. *Yea for me,* he thought. *I beat another one. Stupid damn cops.*

CHAPTER SIX

Barry was sitting, across the desk, from a man named Curt. Curt looked like he had played center linebacker someplace, and somewhere along the line had run into a brick wall. He had very rugged features and a pug nose. It was forty degrees in the trailer and this dude was wearing a tee shirt that showed a very nice physique. His biceps looked as if they might rip his sleeves out if he flexed them.

"So, you haven't worked in four years and you came to Alaska to find work?" This man with the muscles talked softly, sounding nothing like he looked.

"Something like that." Barry was being careful with his answers.

"When did you get here?"

"Four years ago."

"You been mooching off Father Kevin for four years?" he laughed.

Barry laughed, too. "No, I was living off the land for four years—in a cabin about 110 mikes north of here."

"Let's go out back and talk with Mike. He's the straw boss." Curt was done with the questions. *Thank heavens,* Barry thought.

"We can use a laborer out on the red sand project." Mike said. Mike was about fifty, with the ruddy look of a man who had worked outside most of his life. His gray hair was cut short and his glasses gave him a studious look. He shook Barry's hand and said, "Welcome aboard."

Curt and Barry walked back to the office. "Let's start Monday morning," Curt said. "Be here at seven. The pay is twenty dollars an hour, but no benefits, so take care of yourself."

Barry walked back outside, feeling good about how things had gone. The air was crisp, but the sun was shining and melting the snow that had fallen the night before. He owed Father Kevin a big "thank you."

He had four days to waste as it was Thursday afternoon. First, he needed to get himself a wristwatch. He went to a small park down by the river, and sitting on a bench, he reached into his pocket and took Sneaky out into his hand. The little gray mouse looked at him as if to say, "How did we do?"

What was he going to do with Sneaky while he worked? He couldn't take him with, and he was going to be in big trouble if he got caught with him in any rooming house. Maybe it's time to let him go and hope he finds a place to survive, but no, they had come so far, and had been through so much.

He put him back in his pocket, but not before he cleaned out the little leather pouch and gave him some more biscuit to eat. *He'd think of something. Time to go buy that watch.*

Torch had packed a small bag as soon as he got home from the police station. He'd probably only be gone overnight. Stopping down at the desk, he'd had them run a rap sheet on Skip Hendricks, but he was nowhere in the system. Still, something told him he had seen him before.

In the morning, Charlie dropped him off at the airport, kissing him goodbye but holding him for an extra minute before she let go. "Just remember, you old fart, you're not as young as you used to be, so be careful."

Smiling, Torch grabbed her butt and said, "Keep it warm, baby."

Charlie turned red, and looked around to see who was watching them before she giggled and said, "Dirty old man."

It was only about an hour's flight from Minneapolis to Milwaukee. A man in a brown overcoat, with a protruding Adams apple and a narrow face, spotted Torch as he came off the plane. "You don't look like your picture, detective," he said, approaching Torch with his hand outstretched.

"Better or worse?" Torch laughed.

"Don Holtern," he said, shaking hands and ignoring the question. "I have a car waiting for us. The Captain wants to see you before you interview Hendricks, so we will be going downtown and then to the jail. He says he has some additional information you might be happy to know."

"I can use all of the help I can get," Torch answered. The ride in was a quiet one with the two detectives sitting in the back of the squad. Don was on his cell phone most of the way, in a lengthy conversation with what seemed to be a wayward son.

The Captain was more friendly and talkative, and he and Torch hit it off right off the bat. Especially when they found out they had worked together early in their careers.

"What made you leave Minneapolis and go to Milwaukee?" Torch asked.

"I don't really know, Torch. Maybe it was the Packers." He laughed and slapped Torch on the shoulder. "Sit down and let's talk about Skip Hendricks."

Torch slipped off his coat but held it in his lap. The Captain's office was plastered with pictures of Old Green Bay Packers—Bart Star, Paul Horning and Jim Taylor among many.

"Friends?" Torch asked, pointing at the pictures.

"You might say that. I got season tickets and my daughter is engaged to one of them. I get to sit with some of the old greats from time to time."

"I'm impressed," Torch said. "The closest I ever got to the Vikings is when I arrested some of them at a party once. Chief hated me, said it was a public relations headache, and told me I need to look the other way once in a while."

"How did that work out?"

"They all got their fingers slapped and went on their way. I got the shaft."

"Torch, we arrested Skip Hendricks the other night for drunk and disorderly conduct. He tried to piss on a squad car, and when the officer got out and questioned him, he got unruly and the fight started, so we locked him up overnight. The next morning, when we sent an investigator down to question him, the very first thing he said was, 'I'm not guilty of murdering anyone, so all of you dicks can just back off.' We had no idea what he was talking about, but we let him ramble on, and he made the following statement.

'I was found innocent of that murder in North Carolina, and I had nothing to do with that one in Minneapolis, either.' Keep in mind...he was still half in the bag when we questioned him, and wasn't making much sense about anything. Then, just like that, he shut up and hasn't talked since. Right after that, I got a call saying there were warrants out on him from Minneapolis and you guys wanted to talk to him about a DNA match. What's that all about?"

"Well, when he was arrested in North Carolina they took a DNA sample from him, and got a hit on a case that has been in our cold files forever. Can you smoke in here?"

"No, but let's go outside, I could use a heater, too." The captain grabbed his jacket off the back of the chair and the men walked down a long hallway and out into a small courtyard. There were two uniformed officers already out there smoking and they both stuffed out their cigarettes and left.

"Look," Torch said, after they had both lit up. "I was the investigating officer on the murder case where his DNA turned up. We got a conviction on the case on her drunken husband, who I still say did it, but he jumped bail and no one has seen him for the last four years. For ten years or so he was living right under our noses, with another woman and her family. It's a long story, and I'm not going to bore you with the details, but I'm still convinced he did it and we're still looking for him."

"He? You mean the husband?"

"Yes. Not this joker in here that pissed on your squad car. I'm not sure why his DNA turned up at the scene but I'm sure there is an explanation somewhere. By the way, did you get some more DNA when he whizzed on the car?"

He smiled and said "No. Glad it's your case. Well, let's go see him and then we have to kick him loose."

Both men snuffed out their smokes and went back inside. "Jail's on the second floor," the Captain said, and opened the door into a stairwell.

Barry was walking back to the church after buying a watch at the outlet store. He still didn't have enough money to pay for a hotel room, and he wanted to ask the good Father if he could stay there until he got paid.

Father Kevin was in the kitchen doing dishes, when Barry walked in. It was the middle of the afternoon so the place was empty except for a cook, who was stirring something on the stove.

"Father, can I ask you something?" Barry spoke through a half-open serving window into the kitchen. The priest walked over, wiping his hands on a dishtowel, and the cook looked up and wiped her nose on her sleeve. She looked like she was in pain.

"I got the job," Barry said. "Thank you for your help. Now my problem is, I don't have enough money to stay anywhere until I get paid next week."

"That's fine," the priest said. "You can stay here."

"I have some money and I'll pay what I can," Barry said.

"Good. Every little bit helps us. Give me a couple of minutes to finish up in the kitchen and let's talk some more. "I'll get us some coffee."

I wonder what he wants to talk about, Barry thought, as he sat down.

Father Kevin was thinking, too, as he rinsed out the last of the kettles. His shelter wasn't only meant for saving lost bodies from the ravages of the Alaskan winter, it was meant for saving lost souls, too. Most of his clients cared less about his preaching—they only needed a place to sleep and wear off the effects of the cheap wine they lived on, an occasional hot meal, and some strong coffee to wake them up and give them the energy to hit the streets once more, and do what they did best—beg and scrounge for their next drink. They had left Jesus behind them long ago, but out of courtesy for the good padre, they listened to what he had to say but seldom reacted. Father didn't push them, not wanting them to be scared off, either. But Barry seemed different. He was strangely quiet, and to himself, and Father was convinced he was hiding something. There was, however, something Barry had said that gave him some hope he could get to know him better. He had told Father he was Catholic.

Back in Minneapolis, high in the government center and in the halls of justice, Charlie sat in court. She wasn't participating in the case but was observing a new attorney that she had hired, who was trying her first case and so far, she wasn't impressed.

The case involved a hit and run driver who killed an elderly woman, and then fled the scene. The driver was later caught when he tried to get his car fixed and the body shop owner alerted police.

Charlie's new lawyer had given her initial presentation to the jury, and although it should have been an easy case and one she should have aggressively attacked from the get go, she had appeared passive, and lacking the tenacity Charlie expected from her attorneys. Some of it could be explained as inexperience and courtroom jitters, but she wasn't running a school here, she was running a County Attorney's office. Right now, the defense was presenting their case in a long, drawn- out and boring oratory that Charlie had heard many times before.

Her mind, drifting now, was focused on Torch, and why he had wanted to get back into the case he had been so obsessed with. *Old cops*, she reasoned, *like old soldiers, died hard and hers was not ready to roll over quite yet. But it went farther than that. Torch had been involved in many cases that were never resolved or solved but this one was different—or so it seemed.*

The tone of voice had changed and she was aware the defense attorney was sitting down and the judge was now talking.

"We'll continue this tomorrow," he said. "Ten a.m. right here. Is that all right with both of you?"

Neither attorney objected so he pounded his gavel and said, "Court is adjourned." Charlie motioned for her attorney to follow her out into the hall. "Let's get together about four this afternoon and talk about this," she said. The young lady, laden down with papers and her briefcase, nodded her head but said nothing. She knew she hadn't won any points with Charlie.

As she walked back to her office, her thoughts went back to Torch again. *Maybe she should have retired when he did. They had a lot of living left to do.*

Both of them, sitting at the table, had their hands cupped around their coffee mugs as it was cold in the church basement. "What brought you to Alaska, Barry? Not cold enough in Minnesota?"

Barry laughed. "No, I just needed a change of scenery, I guess. I have always been intrigued with life up here and wanted to try it out. I guess, if I were a younger man, I would stay. But right now, I have some business to take care of back in Minnesota. Maybe I'll be back some day. It's nice up here."

"Where have you been living while you were here?"

Barry looked at the priest. *Too damn many questions,* he thought. "About a hundred miles east of here."

"That's rugged country," the priest said.

"Yep, I loved it, and I did well out there, but it's time to get back to civilization."

Father Kevin could see that Barry was reluctant to offer any more information than he had to. "Barry, you mentioned you were Catholic once. Well, I guess for that matter, you still are. Do you miss the church?"

"I'm not sure, Father. I was raised in a good Catholic home, and even went to Catholic school, but it's been a long time since I was faithful."

"It's never too late to come back," he said. "Can I show you the church?"

He's helped me a lot, thought Barry, *and I at least owe him the courtesy of pretending to be interested in his church.*

"Yeah, I'd like that," Barry said. The doors to the upstairs were locked and Father inserted a key he carried on a wristband—not everyone came here to pray.

They walked slowly up a set of stairs to a landing, then took a right turn and went up a few more steps to the Narthex. The gathering area was small and cluttered with tables holding information racks filled with tracts and bulletins about church activities. Just ahead was a set of double glass doors that opened into the church proper.

"It's not a big church, but it has a lot of history. I'm the fourteenth priest who has been blessed to serve here." He pointed to a row of pictures of all the pastors of the parish who had served since the nineteen forties. Some of them looked almost like Moses with their long beards and clerical coats.

As they stepped through the doors into the church, Barry was as nervous as if he was someplace he didn't deserve to be. His thoughts went back to North Minneapolis and the church he was raised in. He remembered how religious and faithful his mother had been, and how she made him learn all of the church prayers. Coming into his bedroom the last thing each night, and tucking him in, and reciting all of them with him.

Interrupting these thoughts, Father Kevin motioned him down the center aisle, genuflected and sat down in a pew a few seats from the front. He patted the seat next to him, asking Barry to sit with him.

"Can you feel the presence of our Lord?" Father asked.

Barry nodded his head, but his attention was being drawn to the elaborate altar. Off to the left was a large statue of the Blessed Virgin Mary. The prayer came back to him in snippets. *Hail Mary full of Grace the Lord is in you...No, the Lord is with you?* Barry remembered all of the rosaries he had prayed with his mother, kneeling on the living room floor by the tattered couch, and how could he ever forget that prayer.

Just then, Sister Joanna came down the aisle and whispered something to Father. "I'll be right back, Barry," he said.

Suddenly, Barry realized he was all alone—or was he? He was in the presence of the Lord, was he not? He should say something. After all, he was in a church, was he not, and God was listening. *I hope he's listening,* he thought. *I've given him lots of reasons to write me off.* Maybe he should kneel and say it. Show a little reverence. Slowly, he went to his knees, folded his hands together and bowed his head.

Lord, I'm so sorry, he prayed. *Help me to do the right thing.*

Barry stood up again, and then, gazing at the altar one last time, he walked out of the church and back down the stairs. He was feeling strangely calm. Something he hadn't felt in a long time.

Father Kevin, on the phone in the back of the church, saw him leave. He also saw a more serene look on Barry's face rather than the suspicious scowl that was usually there. *Maybe it's a start,* he thought. *We take in a lot of destitute people here and sometimes you get the chance to not only save a life, but save a soul, too.*

There was something about Barry that Father Kevin couldn't let go of. Barry seemed to be hiding something, but nothing jumped out at him. He would have to proceed cautiously so as not to make him suspicious. If he could bring him back to the church, that would be a good start. They really had nothing in common except they were both from Minneapolis. But Barry didn't know that, did he? Not yet, anyway.

CHAPTER SEVEN

Torch and Skip were sitting at a small table, in an interview room down the hall from the jail. Skip was unkempt with shaggy, gray, greasy blond hair, and a mouth full of rotten teeth, and was making sucking sounds with his tongue in his teeth. His head was down but he was looking up at Torch through the tops of his bloodshot eyes.

"Hi, I'm Torch Brennan," he said. "I heard you were here and wanted to talk to you."

"Are you a cop?" Skip said, in a raspy voice.

"I was a cop, but I'm retired right now."

"So how come you're here?"

"I just wanted to ask you some questions."

"About what?"

Torch noticed there was an ashtray on the table, and reaching in his shirt pocket, took out his pack of smokes and offered one to Skip.

"Thanks," Skip said, lighting the smoke with Torch's lighter and inhaling deeply.

"Keep the pack," Torch said, and pushed them across the table. "Skip, when you were living in Minneapolis years ago where did you work?"

"Who said I lived In Minneapolis? I live in North Carolina."

"You haven't always lived there," Torch said, "and I can prove it. Let's just quit the games and be truthful here."

"You working for the cops?"

"No, I'm working for myself, and I'll ask the questions here. Who did you work for in Minneapolis in 1991?"

Skip looked up at Torch, one eye closed from the cigarette smoke drifting from his lips to his eye. "I worked for a courier delivering packages."

"Which courier?" Torch said, sounding more forceful.

"Flagg's—they were a small firm over Nord East."

This statement caught Torch's attention. No one said, "Nord East" except people who lived there. "Skip, the other night when you were booked you made the following statement. 'I was found innocent of that murder in North Carolina and I had nothing to with the one in Minneapolis.'"

"I said that?" Skip looked astonished.

"Yeah, you said that and more, and it's on tape. Want to hear it?"

"No, I want a lawyer."

"You're not going to talk to me anymore?"

Skip shook his head but said nothing.

Torch picked up his pack of cigarettes and walked out.

Torch was back in the Captain's office. "He lawyered up on me. Anyway, can you hold him a few more days?"

"You got a charge? Otherwise, no."

"Well, Captain, right now I personally can't arrest him, but let me talk to Ray back in the cities. Give me a few minutes, okay?"

Torch went out in the hallway and then, not getting a cell phone signal, he went back out on the patio.

"Homicide. Detective Ray Walton."

"Ray, it's Torch…here in Milwaukee. I just got done talking with Hendricks and I don't know what to think. Before I got around to asking him about the murder, or mentioning the DNA evidence, he shut up and asked for a lawyer. He did say some incriminating things, but not to me. I would like to talk with him some more, but they're kicking him loose here."

Ray asked Torch, "So what do you want me to do?"

"Put out a warrant for his arrest and extradite him back to Minneapolis."

"What if he doesn't want to come back, and what evidence do I have to charge him with?"

The DNA evidence and the statement he made here to the Milwaukee police."

"What was that statement he made?"

"He said, 'he never had anything to do with any murder in Minneapolis.' His words, Ray, and no one asked him about anything in Minneapolis."

Ray let out a short whistle. "Okay. You tell the Captain to hold him until tonight and I'll get a warrant ready, if I can find a judge today. I'll fax it to him. You might as well bring him back with you, if he doesn't fight extradition."

"Can I do that without a badge?"

"Ah shit, I forgot. Well, ask the Captain to send an officer with you. Tell him I'll pick up the tab. If he fights extradition they can keep him locked up there until the hearing."

Torch stomped out the butt of the smoke he had been enjoying. *Better quit this before I go to a full-blown habit again*, he thought. *Charlie will kick my ass if she knows.* He headed back to the Captain's office.

It was Sunday, the day before he started his job. Barry had breakfast and then offered to wash dishes for Sister Joanna while she was at Mass. He had given some thought about going to Mass himself, and then changed his mind. Father Kevin had gotten him thinking about his faith a little, but he wasn't ready for that yet. *Too many sins,* he thought.

He was just finishing up the last of the kettles when the priest walked into the kitchen. "Missed you at Mass," he said.

Barry looked up at the young priest. "I'm not there yet, Father, but I'm thinking about it. Maybe next Sunday. I've got a lot of baggage."

"If its sin you're talking about, I've got a way to get rid of it."

Barry wiped his hands on his pants, and said, "Maybe later, Father."

I hope so, my friend, I really hope so, he thought, as Barry grabbed his coat and went outside.

The young priest went to his office to work on a homily for next week. Never in his wildest dreams had he thought he would get a parish in this frozen land. But he came from an order of missionaries, and although their headquarters was in Minneapolis, they had been sent all over the world to preach the Word of God. Minnesota had cold winters, too, but nothing like this.

That night, the Northern Lights lit up the sky as never before. They seemed to shimmer and shake in a kaleidoscope of colors, as if they were oozing from the backside of the mountains far to the north. Barry sat on the steps outside of the church, knowing he should get to sleep, but not wanting to miss anything. What a beautiful land this was—so far away from the crime and pollution that plagued the big cities in the lower forty-eight.

Something was happening to him, and maybe it was the Spirit of God. Maybe it was just that he was weary of not being a free man, but at the same time, he didn't want to do something worse in retribution than what he had been accused of doing, and was being hunted for. There had to be a way to resolve this and give him something to hang his hat on.

Maybe it was time to lay it out in front of God and get some help. But how? The minute he showed his face back in Minneapolis they would lock him up. There seemed to be only one answer. The only way they were going to believe him was for him to solve the crime. He had to find the person or persons who had killed her and he didn't have a clue whom that could be. Or did he? He just knew it wasn't him. It was time to confide in Father Kevin. He needed all the help he could get.

Slowly, Barry walked up the steps, through the doors, and down to the basement. Tomorrow was a big day.

Ray had found a judge, and through some convincing talk, had gotten his warrant and faxed it to Milwaukee. A Milwaukee County sheriff's deputy would accompany Torch and Hendricks back to Minneapolis. Skip was still not talking to anyone.

Skip knew damn well what they were talking about, and he remembered that night as if it had happened only yesterday. *He watched them coming home from a party that night, in the shelter of his car parked across the street. He had driven by here so many times before. Barry was so drunk she had half-carried him into the house. Skip left his car, and went around to the patio doors that came off their bedroom. For a while he stayed in the safety of some bushes. He had arrived outside the bedroom about the same time that Kim had turned on the light, and poured Barry into the bed. She took off his shoes and pants, her back to Skip and the patio doors. Otherwise, she* left him dressed. Then she went back to the other side of the bed, and took off her clothes, slowly and methodically, as if she was putting on a show for her drunken husband, but in reality, was putting the show on for Skip. She went to the dresser and selected a pair of pajamas but she didn't put them on. She just lay on the bed, on her side, nude and fondled her drunken husband as if she was trying to bring it back to life. Gradually, she gave up and took care of things herself in a slow and sensual act.

He could never forget her fondling herself, and he could never forget how beautiful and perfectly formed she was. She was just as he had imagined her to be in his fantasies. She'd always smiled so nicely and thanked him when he left off the packages at the shop; bending over to sign his clipboard, and giving him a look down her blouse.

At last, she slipped off to sleep, the pajamas still on the end of the bed. The lamp still on beside the bed.

Skip was so wrought up with sexual desire he was out of his mind. He had to see her closer. She was just so damn beautiful. He went around the house and tried the front door. It was not only unlocked, it was partway open. Carefully, he let himself in. A light above the sink was still on, dimly lighting the kitchen and the butcher-block knife rack that sat on an otherwise clean and empty counter.

He took the knife because he was scared. He had no intention of hurting anyone. In the bedroom, Barry snored loudly as Skip knelt beside the bed on Kim's side. Her legs were slightly spread and Skip bent over her to get a better look at the place his mind was fixated on. The place he had fantasized over so many times. He couldn't see her face because she was holding a pillow to her chest.

That's when her eyes opened, and she tried to sit up. At first, she said nothing, and just stared at him wide-eyed. He panicked and grabbed the pillow she had been hugging, and held it over her face to muffle her screaming. Her legs were flailing out, kicking at him. He held it there until she passed out.

He remembered quickly looking over at Barry, who was still snoring as if nothing had happened.

Kim was still alive—she had recognized him before he rendered her unconscious. Now he was getting scared. She knew him from work. She would call the cops and he would go to jail for sure. He took the knife in his hand, and with no hesitation, slit her throat. The *knife was razor sharp and he could see the array of blood vessels and cords inside of the bloody slit it left. Her quivering hand went up and grabbed the back of his head briefly, as if to pull him closer, then it was over and she went limp.*

There was so much blood. It had squirted everywhere—spraying all over the bed and Barry, too. The coppery stench was overwhelming. He stepped back to get his bearings and get out of that nauseating smell. Then the spurting stream subsided, and nearly stopped, and it was just oozing out, down her neck and into the bedclothes.

Skip had felt strangely calm after killing her. Why had she woken up? Why had he come in there? He still didn't have that answer. He wasn't going to rape her. He took the pajamas off the end of the bed and dressed her. He couldn't stand to see her naked, anymore. The knife was still nearby, where he could reach it in case her drunken slob of a husband woke up. Then he stabbed her in the chest many more times, and then buttoned up her pajama top, which was still open, putting the bloody knife in her husband's hand, but not before he wiped his prints off the handle, on her pajama top. Then he let himself out the patio door. It was pouring rain outside.

The squeal of tires, as the plane hit the runway, signaled that the short trip from Milwaukee to Minneapolis was over. Torch told Skip, "Just stay seated, buddy. We're the last to get off."

"Got no place to go, anyway," Skip muttered.

"Yes, you do, my friend. Yes, you do," Torch said, looking out the window as they approached the gate. In the distance, he could see the Minneapolis squad waiting for them.

Torch turned to the deputy. "Thanks for the help, buddy. I owe you a beer sometime."

"Maybe a Wisconsin beer," he laughed. "Good luck with your new friend."

CHAPTER EIGHT

The work was hard, and was made harder because Barry was out of shape. By noon, he had worn out the fingertips of his new gloves from carrying the rough cement blocks to the block layers. Most Alaskan's were used to working half the day in darkness, and with the approach of winter, it seemed to be getting colder by the day.

By the end of the workday he was tired, cold and hungry. He couldn't get back to the church fast enough. He was going to sleep good tonight. He ate in silence, sitting by himself until the familiar face of Father Kevin appeared, carrying a tray, and asking if he could sit down.

Barry smiled, and motioned to the empty chair.

"Hard day?" the priest asked.

"Yeah, I'm not in very good shape when it comes to manual labor, but I'll be all right. I'm surprised to see you here. I would have guessed you would have a housekeeper who made you pot roast and homemade bread most nights."

"No...no," he laughed. "Most nights I eat right here. I have no housekeeper and I'm a lousy cook. Why, is the food that bad?"

"No!" Barry almost shouted. "The food is good and I'm thankful for it. It's the best I've eaten in years. I just thought...oh, never mind."

Father Kevin laughed. "Barry, I know what you meant. I was just yanking your chain a little. Sister is a good cook."

For a few minutes there was an awkward silence, and then the young priest broke the ice. "Barry, from the first moment I met you I had the feeling you were running from something. Would you like to talk about it?"

It was as if an alarm bell had gone off in the back of his head. *Was this man really his friend or not? How could he have possibly found out about his past?* "I think your intuition is betraying you, Father. I have no sordid past to talk about, and if I did, I wouldn't talk about it here." *I'm lying to a priest*, he thought.

"Not everyone runs from the past, Barry. Some of us run from the future. But let's drop the subject, and talk about getting you back on the right side of God. Let's go upstairs, if you're done eating. That's an invitation, Barry, not an order."

They took their trays back to the kitchen, and then both of the men walked up the stairs to the church.

Torch was going to go home to Charlie. In the morning, he would go see Ray with his ideas. He had a couple of thoughts about something that he might have missed in the first investigation, but basically, he still thought Barry did it. Until something more convincing happened, it was going to stay that way.

They sat in the front pew looking at the altar. Father Kevin was sitting sideways, looking right at Barry. "I want to help you, Barry, but you need to tell me the truth. I'm not insinuating you haven't been truthful, I just want you to know this is serious business with me."

"Father, when someone makes a confession to you, you can't divulge that, right?"

"That's right, Barry, and if you want this conversation in the form of a confession, we can do that."

Barry didn't respond to the statement Father Kevin make, but he went on to say, "I trust you. You have every right to be suspicious of me. I'm wanted by the law back in Minnesota."

"For what?" Father asked.

"I was accused of killing my wife, but Father, sitting here right now in front of him, he looked up at the crucifix, and you, in this holy place, as God is my witness...I did not do it."

"Tell me about it," Father said.

For the next hour Barry bared his soul. Father Kevin listened intently to each and every word. Barry went back to the night of the murder, and the twenty years since. He talked about the dreams he had, and how real they seemed but yet, somehow, they didn't give him the clue he needed.

He talked about how much he had loved Kim, and how he would have never harmed her. "She was my, life my everything," he whispered. He talked about how much hate he had for the Minneapolis Police Department, and especially Torch Brennan, the detective who had pursued him so relentlessly.

When he was done talking, Barry seemed spent. He had wanted to share this story for twenty years, with someone who would believe him and listen to him, and now he'd shared it, but did the man really believe him.

"I came from Minneapolis, too. They have a seminary there for the order I belong to. I'm not familiar with your wife's murder, although I must have been there at about that time. Is the case still active?"

"Active? They never give up, Father. Unlike your profession, there is no forgiveness."

"Look, Barry. Let me think about this for a while. I have friends in Minneapolis yet. But I don't want to say or do anything that would tip off your whereabouts."

Barry didn't answer him; he just stared at the cleric, his eyes filling with tears.

Father Kevin put his hand on Barry's shoulder. "I do believe you, Barry," he said softly. "Let's talk again in a few days."

When Barry left the church, Father Kevin continued to sit in the front pew, thinking about all that he had heard. He had a bustling parish to run, with a lot of activities. There were the sick to visit, weddings and funerals to officiate at. Just feeding and housing the homeless and poor took a lot of time. But once in awhile, something came along he couldn't let go of, and this was one of those times. He wanted to help Barry.

Tonight he would call his friend and former teacher, Father Tim Monk, who was, as far as he knew, still the Chaplin for the Minneapolis Police Department. He needed to find out more about Barry, and if he was still being actively pursued.

Father Kevin turned himself around in the pew, facing the altar, and went to his knees. When things became difficult, or he was somewhat befuddled, it always helped to talk to the boss. He asked God for guidance and understanding, and if he could help Barry, that it would be made possible. But most of all, he asked that Barry be brought back into the church and would, himself, place his trust in God.

Two things had impressed the young priest about Barry's story. First, it was his sincerity. Over the years as a priest, listening to so many people and hearing so many confessions, he had developed a sense for when people were being forthright with him. Kevin felt Barry was not being deceitful with him, and he genuinely wanted the truth to come out. The other thing that had grabbed his attention there, in that pew, and probably the most important thing to him, was Barry talking about the dreams he had experienced over the years, of that night when his wife was murdered. He had taken many psychology classes in college; in fact, he had a B.A. degree in it. Besides being a steward, and teacher of the Catholic faith, he had a great understanding of the working of the human mind. This man was not a sociopath, and for someone to murder someone as Barry had described it, well, they had to be pretty sick. It always intrigued him how secrets, that were locked away in the dark recesses of the brain, could sometimes be let loose with the right techniques, and God willing, that was something they would have to work on if they wanted the truth. He made the sign of the cross and left to go back to his office. He had other work to do.

Torch was given some office space, and a computer to use, in what once was an old janitor's closet. He wanted to settle this case one way or another. He still felt Barry had done it. Proving Skip could have been at the scene did not prove that Skip had anything to do with it, but it didn't answer the question why he would lie and say he had never had contact with Kim if, in fact, that was what he was going to say.

Skip still wasn't talking. He had been given a public defender, who was demanding that Torch show him what evidence he had, because he knew it was flimsy at best and he wanted to get bail set for his client or, at the least, have the charges dropped.

Flagg's Courier service wasn't in business anymore, at least, not as Flagg's. They had been bought out two years ago, and now were part of a larger service called Twin City Parcel Services. Torch asked for, and was granted, permission to come and talk to their record department and personnel manager.

The building was a one-story gray office building along Olsen Memorial Highway in Minneapolis, where it had moved from Northeast, and it looked as if it was a prosperous business. The lawn was well kept up, and the ivy-covered building appeared to be almost new. It looked out of place in this part of town, which was not known for being in the best part of the city. There was a lot of crime and ethnic problems in the area.

Torch was meeting with Ms. Melinda Oaks, who headed up the record-keeping department, along with human services. Melinda was well kept for an older lady when it came to her personal appearance, but it was obvious she had been around this earth for a long time. She seemed to be quite poised and in charge of herself. She wore her glasses on a gold chain around her neck, and her long red hair was stacked up on top of her head. She welcomed Torch into her office, and asked if he wanted a cup of coffee.

"I'm all coffee'd out, but thank you," he said.

"I'm always ready and willing to do what I can to help the police department," she said. "Now, detective, what can I do for you?" She was playing with the crease in the pant leg of her black pantsuit as they both sat in front of the desk. Her long legs were crossed and slung over each other—almost as an invite to say, "Look at these gams." She had a ring on every finger and enough bracelets around her wrist to open her own jewelry store.

Torch looked, for a second, like he had lost his train of thought, but quickly snapped out of it. "I'm looking for some information on a former employee."

She uncrossed and recrossed her legs. "That shouldn't be a problem, unless you want to get into personal information that we can't release."

"No. No, I don't think that's the case. But for starters, let's make sure he worked here. His name was Skip Hendricks, and the time I'm interested in was about twenty years ago."

"Well, that's going back a ways, so why don't you give me a day or so. Did he work for this company? I mean, did he work for Twin City Parcel or Flagg's? "If it was twenty years ago it had to be Flagg's."

"He said it was Flagg's."

She was writing all of this down. "We have most of Flagg's information on file, but it might take some digging. Do you have a number that I can use to get back to you?"

Torch handed her an old business card; one of many that he had used before he retired. The number had changed, so he had crossed it out and put in his current number. "That's my cell," he said.

"Does this…" she looked at the name she had written down "… Skip Hendricks." She stopped, "I guess what I was going to say is, is he in any trouble with the law?"

"Not that I can talk about right now," Torch answered. "I'm just trying to see if he worked here back then. If he did, then I might be able to give you a better explanation."

Ms. Oaks seemed a little miffed. She was usually the one who withheld information, and she wasn't used to being put off. "Okay," she said. "I will get back to you."

When Torch left the office, for a moment he thought about going back down to police headquarters, and then reasoned that there was nothing more to do there until he got more information. No, it was time to go home and see his wife. He was tired, and was already regretting that he had gotten involved again in this investigation. There had been a reason he had retired in the first place, and now that he had refreshed his memory, it was all coming back to him. *It hadn't been just the bureaucracy that he talked about when people asked him why he retired. It had been the frustration that comes with talking to lying people. He felt that he had proved that Barry Winston killed his wife. If he didn't, then fine. Let him prove he was innocent.*

Father Kevin had his doubts, and was having second thoughts, too, about trying to help Barry out. He hadn't been able to get in touch with Father Monk back in Minneapolis. Seemed he was in Rome on a sabbatical. Father Kevin's job was to spread the Gospel of Jesus Christ here in Fairbanks, and to try and feed the poor and heal their spirits and bodies. His time was already stretched thin, and now he was thinking about getting involved in this man's problems. This wasn't the first time he had done this, but some of his other trips into uncharted waters had gone bad for him. He needed to talk with Barry once more before he continued.

CHAPTER NINE

The work was hard, but each day it became easier as Barry worked himself into shape. He became good friends with a few of the other guys, even to the point of eating with them, and stopping after work for a beer. He listened to their stories of their family's affairs, and could only smile softly, as he had no stories of his own. None he could share anyway.

He would be forty-three in a few days, which was half of his life span, if he was lucky. Nothing to show for it but a pile of warrants back in Minnesota, and the loss of the only woman he had ever loved. It was getting harder and harder to see the sunlight as winter set in, in December, in Fairbanks. He started work at seven in the dark, and went back to the church each night at four thirty in the dark. It was hard to be upbeat.

Since that day in the front pew in the church, Barry was more at ease around Father Kevin. Yes, he had some skeletons in his closet, but he trusted Father with them. Last night they had eaten together again, and Father told him about a problem they were having at the church. With the advent of the cold weather, more and more homeless people were crowding in each night. "Maybe it's time for you to look for a room elsewhere," he told him. "No hurry, Barry. Take your time, but I do need your bed."

He had known this conversation would be coming, and right now he had the money to pay his own way so maybe it was time, and no one knew more than he what it was like to not have a place to stay. Today was Friday and payday. Tomorrow he would go looking, but for tonight he was bushed and just wanted to get to bed. Also, he had a very sore spot on his back, which was unusual for him.

Ms. Oaks called Torch on Monday and told him, "Yes, Skip had worked for Flagg's for three years, driving delivery truck." He had been let go in the spring of 1993 for reasons she couldn't tell him, "Unless you have a warrant," she said. Torch couldn't help thinking that was payback, for him not telling her what kind of trouble Skip was in, when she was being nosy yesterday. *Well, he would fix her bony ass,* he thought to himself. He planned on getting a warrant.

On Tuesday he was back out to her office with the warrant in hand. She made him wait for over an hour, but at last, her secretary let him in. "Ms. Oaks will see you now, Mr. Brennan."

"Call me Torch," he said, with a smile.

She smiled back, but didn't say anything more.

She read the warrant carefully, and then asked Torch, "What is it you need to know, detective?"

"I need to know why Skip Hendricks was fired, and I need to know the exact time he worked for Flagg's." She went back to the papers she had on her desk. "Mr. Hendricks worked here from January 1990 until April of ninety-three. He was fired because there was a complaint against him by a female employee that he had tried to rape her."

"Were the police involved in this?" Torch asked.

"Not to my knowledge, because the woman refused to file a complaint against him."

"What is her name, and does she still work here?"

"Her name is Doris Malone, and yes, she still works for us. At that time her name was Doris Hendricks."

"Hendricks? Related or just a coincident?"

"She was his wife."

"Wife! Who the hell rapes his own wi…." He left the sentence in mid-air. "How do I get a hold of her?"

Ms. Oaks wrote some numbers down on a piece of paper. "Here's her home phone and address. I would rather you not bother her here."

Torch took of his hat and scratched his head. "Okay, if you say so. Thanks for the information."

He walked out of the office into the crisp December air. The sun shining bright off the snow made him squint, and he used his hand for a visor to shield his eyes. He had a headache and he wanted to go home, but he needed to go down to headquarters first and do some file digging.

Father Kevin had decided, for the time being, to stay out of Barry's problem. He did want to try something, though. He had a friend in town that worked at a clinic that specialized in hypnosis. Barry's stories about his dreams interested the priest. Barry appeared to be very sincere, and Father's years of hearing confessions made him good at judging that. This friend of his helped a lot of his patients through hypnosis, and was quite good at digging out the demons that plagued them. Maybe those missing pieces of Barry's dreams, from that night, could be retrieved. It wouldn't just help Barry—it would go a long way towards helping the young priest believe Barry's story. First of all, he would have to ask Barry if he would agree to do it, because he would need to be one hundred percent on board with this if it was going to work. They weren't playing games here. He would see Barry tonight. He knew Barry was looking for a place of his own, but right now his stuff was still here at the church, including Sneaky, who slept in a little tin box in Barry's backpack. No longer a secret, Father had agreed that the mouse was important to him so it could stay here with him. He even fed and watered it sometimes when Barry was gone.

Deep in the "cold files room," Torch found the box he was looking for. It simply said, *Kim Winston.* Inside the box were more photographs of the scene. They were dated April fifth of 1992. Some he didn't even remember and he wondered if someone had added pictures he hadn't seen, but that didn't seem plausible. He had worked harder on that case than most of the ones he worked on. He set the pictures aside for the moment.

There was a rape kit that said, "No evidence of sperm was present, but her vagina was bruised and looked as if it had been handled roughly." *Would she have allowed her husband to treat her like that?* He set that aside, too.

The knife that was used was still there in its plastic bag; dried blood was still present on the blade and the handle. He remembered the fingerprints that were the strongest evidence in the case, and they had been Barry's. Not just one set, but several sets, as if he had relaxed his grip and then repositioned his hand, and started in again. The jury had been very interested in that fact. *Had someone else just put the knife in Barry's unconscious hand, that would have been hard to duplicate and who in that state of mind would do that?*

Then, there was Kim's pajama top and bottoms—still stained with dried blood. There had been no knife slits in the cloth so it was surmised, at the trial, that Barry dressed her after he killed her. Also, most of the blood was on the inside of the cloth. It had seemed that an outsider would have never taken the time to dress his victim; but a husband, worried about his wife's vanity, would have. Yes, all of the theories and facts were coming back to him. He took the pajamas out of their bag and laid them on the table in front of him. He remembered, when the body was photographed, how they were buttoned up wrong. Not really much of a clue, but a fact to think about.

There was a coroner's photo showing the stab wounds, and when you laid the pajama top out, the bloody spots corresponded to the wounds, and that made sense. The collar was soaked in blood from her neck wound. She had been found on her back and the blood had pooled around her neck and that, too, made sense. This wasn't the first time he and other detectives had gone over this, although it had been twenty years ago.

As Torch folded the pajama top to put it back in the bag, he noticed a smear of blood on the right sleeve. There were many places that blood had run and collected in the bed but this spot didn't seem to fit and it wasn't a spot of blood but more of a smear. It was on the shoulder of the sleeve, on her right side. The front of the shoulder and he wasn't so sure this one wasn't on the outside of the cloth to start with. Torch pulled up a chair and sat down. *If she was nude when this happened, then how did the blood get in this spot? There was no corresponding wound to this blood spot and blood eking out of wounds after she was dressed would not have been on top of her shoulder. It was too far from her neck and the worst wound. It didn't look like a spray of blood but more of a smear as if something had been wiped off.* This was way too obvious of a clue not to have been noticed in the original investigation. He needed to find out what had been said about this way back then. It had probably already been explained, but after all of these years he didn't remember it.

Torch bagged the pajama top back up. He was going to have it sent to the lab to find out if the blood was on the inside, and soaked through, or was it on the outside to start with. *Something didn't fit here, and how had he missed this in the original investigation? Or had he?* He needed to read his old notes. It was time to get home. Charlie would be home by now, and they hadn't seen much of each other lately.

Barry was starting to like Fairbanks despite the cold weather. He had been raised in Minnesota, and although it was not Fairbanks, it did get cold there, too. He had found a small efficiency apartment that was just the right size for a single man, and he was having a phone installed. He had bought an old birdcage, and now Sneaky had his own home in a warm sunny location—when the sun was shining. Things at work were going good. He had made many friends amongst the block and bricklayers, and sometimes, the bosses let him do some framing. He would always be a carpenter at heart. He missed Father Kevin and their talks, and had taken to going to Mass on Sundays just to stay in touch. It wasn't, however, just the priest he was trying to stay in touch with. His faith was also being revived.

That nagging desire to go back to Minneapolis, and get his pound of flesh, was slowly ebbing. Yes, it was something he still wanted to do but maybe, for a while, it would be good to just live as a common man for a change.

He still had the nagging pain in his back, but it seemed to come and go. The one thing he didn't have was health insurance, or he would have gone to the doctor and had it checked out. He needed all of his money to get into a vehicle. Walking or taking buses was starting to suck. But first, he was going to get an Alaska driver's license, and that presented a problem. Back in Minnesota, there were warrants out for his arrest. Did their tentacles stretch as far as Fairbanks?

So far, Barry had avoided paying taxes where he worked because he had hired on as a temporary person, and was paid in cash. Not paying taxes avoided the documents that would have had his social security number on them. That, too, was soon going to be a problem. The other day at work, Curt had said that, "it was getting time to make things legal."

How could he avoid all of this? He didn't know, but maybe Father Kevin had an idea—he was always coming up with answers. He would bring it up to him, but first he was going to go to Mass tomorrow morning. He needed help, and he wasn't going to get it here unless he sought some form of divine intervention. *It's funny,* he mused, *how people always come back to God when all of their other options seem to be exhausted.* Even that, though, seemed to be out of character for him. My, how he was changing.

Sunday morning dawned cold and windy. The fog rolled off the river as the warmer water met the cold air. Barry walked the mile down to the church, by the river, hoping two things would happen. One, that somehow he could revive the faith he had left behind him so long ago. It seemed odd to him that he would want that to happen after decades of getting along without God's help. And two, that right now he would have a purpose in life beyond staying alive. He was tired of living in anger and hate. He had wasted too much of life already, and now he wanted the rest of it to matter, if to no one else other than him. What was it the *Prayer of Serenity* said? "To accept the things he could not change." Here he was, the refugee from the wild and a fugitive from the grasp of justice, reciting old prayers he had, remarkably, never forgotten. There were about fifty people in church when he walked in and sat down in the last pew, holding his hat in his lap, Mass was just beginning.

Father Kevin noticed him right away, but tried not to make it too obvious. He was more interested in Barry's reactions to being there than anything. He seemed to be listening, but looked like he was self-conscious. He didn't sing, but he followed the prayers. He didn't look right. His complexion was darker and he seemed to be in pain—stretching his arm as if something was cramping, but he was sitting way in the back and it was hard to see him clearly. He'd try to talk to him after Mass.

As the service concluded, and Father Kevin made his way to the back of the church, he noticed that Barry was gone.

Barry was making his way home to his small apartment. He had enjoyed the service and was glad he had gone, but he just wished he felt better. Whatever was wrong with him was fast ruining his digestive system, and right now he was very nauseous. He ducked behind a hedge and vomited, but he hadn't eaten anything this morning so all that came up was some bile. It was the third time he had thrown up since last night. This wasn't the flu.

Charlie caught him smoking in the garage. "I am beginning to regret you going back to work, Torch," she said.

Torch knew what she was talking about, and looked down at the cigarette he had tried to conceal in his now-smoking hand. He was like a little boy with his hand in the cookie jar, and he wasn't even going to try and explain. He'd change the subject.

"I found something interesting in the evidence box from that old case I'm working on. I was looking for anything I might have missed way back then, and when I was looking at her pajamas, there was a blood stain that didn't seem to match up with her wounds."

"How so?" Charlie asked.

"Well, we know she wasn't wearing anything when she was stabbed, and she was dressed afterwards. That's something Barry would have done because no man wants some horny cops looking at his wife like that—nude and all." He dropped the cigarette and crushed it out. "There was a smear of blood on the front of the shoulder where it looked like something was wiped off. A place she could have reached with her hands, which by the way, were covered with blood but didn't look like they had been wiped off."

"So...are you saying the knife was wiped off?"

"Could be, counselor...could be. I sent it to the lab to see what they will have to say about it."

"So, detective, what does that prove?" She was giving him back some of his sarcasm while she sorted through a bag of papers."

"Well, for one thing, think back to the last time you stabbed someone. Would you wipe off the knife when you were done?"

"You're going to find out if you don't quit smoking," she said, still rummaging through the newspapers.

"What in the hell are you looking for?" Torch asked.

"My Sunday coupons, detective. You got any clues?"

"You'll have to talk to my lawyer about that," Torch said.

CHAPTER TEN

It was called the Greater Fairbanks Psychiatric Clinic. Dr. Bob Holden had helped a lot of people through his hypnosis treatments, and now he was sitting behind his desk listening to his friend, Father Kevin, talk about Barry.

"Who is this guy and where did he come from?"

Father Kevin lifted up his ball cap and ran his hand through his hair, as if he was smoothing out his thought process. He didn't look very priestly today, dressed in an old hooded sweatshirt and a Minnesota Twins cap. "He came into town a couple of months ago, and was looking for a place to stay, so we put him up for a while. He found work with a construction company, and last week he moved into his own apartment. None of this has anything to do with why I am here. I'm just filling in some details."

"So why are you here?"

"Bob, what I am going to tell you has to be confidential. Okay?"

"Well, he's not my client yet, and that's where it does get confidential, but work around the edges."

"He is running from the law for something he says he didn't do, and I believe him. That's all I can tell you about it."

"Is it a serious crime?" Bob had a habit of getting a lot of furrows in his prominent brow when he asked questions.

"Yes, it's very serious."

"So…I'm getting lost here. How can I help him?"

"By unlocking his mind. He thinks that the real culprit's identity is hidden in his subconscious. He was there when it happened. He has had dreams about it, but they never get him where he wants to be."

"What happened, Father?"

"The crime."

"Look...Kevin...Father. I'm not going to turn the guy in, and I'm not going to share what you told me. What was he accused of?"

The priest was quiet for a second, thinking. *He was on shaky ground here. What Barry told him had been confessed to him in a confession, and the church said it must stay with him and him alone. He was dammed if he did, and dammed if he didn't.*

Finally, looking up from his lap he said, sheepishly, "He was accused of killing his wife," he said. "He woke up in bed and his wife was lying beside him—dead. She had been stabbed many times, and the knife was in his hand when he woke up. He had been passed out drunk, and claims the knife was put there in his hand, and call me crazy, but I believe him. So help me God, if you tell anyone about this..."

"Whoa, Father. Let's get him in here and let me talk to him before you involve me any deeper." He was paging through an appointment book. "I can see him tomorrow after four."

Father Kevin walked out of the clinic and into a snowstorm. He would go see Barry tonight.

Skip was sitting in the Hennepin country jail, and he knew why, but he also knew if he kept his mouth shut they probably had nothing on him. Yes, it had been a big mistake to say what he had said back in Wisconsin; but that wasn't enough to convict him of anything. Sooner or later that old detective was going to talk to him again and he knew that. *I wonder why he's ignoring me now*, he thought. *He didn't bring me back here just to chat about old times.*

By the next day Barry had recovered somewhat, but he still had a lot of pain in his back. It was high in the back on his right side. He was going to give it just a few more days and then he was going to the doctor, money or not. He couldn't work like this because he was getting weaker every day, and so he called in sick for the second day in a row. He also called the church, and left his number for Father Kevin.

Father Kevin had called back a few minutes later, and wanted to see him this morning. That was where he was going right now. He pushed his hands deep in his pockets for warmth, and with his collar pulled up, walked slowly down to the church. It would be good to see his friend.

It was warm in the church when they went in and sat in the last pew—away from the listening ears of Father Kevin's secretary. They shared the same office, and when Father wanted privacy, he usually escaped to the church.

"Man, Barry, you look like shit."

Barry smiled. He had never heard Father swear before, and it caught him off guard.

"Feel like shit, too, Father."

The priest was concerned, but he changed the subject. "Barry, I talked to an old friend of mine about your dreams. He seems to think maybe he can help you find out if there is something hidden deep in your mind. That's his line of work."

"Is he going to turn me in to the cops?"

"No, he keeps things confidential. It's kind of like talking to a lawyer." *Or maybe going to confession with your priest,* he thought. What he had done was going to bother him for a long time.

"What have you told him?" Barry asked.

"Only that you need to unlock your mind and find some answers."

"When? I have no insurance." Barry was shivering despite the warmth of the church. His fever was coming back.

"I'll take care of it, Barry. He wants to see you tomorrow. Here's his business card."

"I don't know, Father. I'm scared that I might find out I did it after all."

"Put it in God's hands, Barry. Let him know if you're not coming, though. Now…what's wrong with your health?"

"I don't know. It's like I have the flu and can't get rid of it. Some days are better than others, and I think I'm getting well, and then it comes back again."

"Let me know if you can't kick it and I'll put you in touch with a doctor. You've lost weight."

Barry didn't answer him. He just wanted to go home and get in bed. He took the card and slipped it in his pocket. He had to get out of here.

Torch was looking at the lab report. It had taken three days and he wanted to talk with Skip again, but not until he had those results, and not until he had the opportunity to talk to one Doris Malone.

She lived in a small townhouse development, in a northern suburb called Brooklyn Center. It was one of the inner ring suburbs of Minneapolis, and if not for the street signs, you would never know when you left Minneapolis and entered Brooklyn Center. She was in her early fifties now, and still single except for a cat named Louis. She was a loner and liked it that way. Even at work she did her job, but rarely had anything to do with the other employees. Last week there had been a Christmas party at work, and she had been the only one not to attend.

When Torch had called her, at first she had been reluctant to talk with him, but after Torch explained the situation, and mentioned Skip Hendricks, she invited him out to her place. It was if she had an axe to grind, but she still wanted to be cautious. She had continued to work for the company all these years.

Torch parked in the cul-de-sac that spread out in front of the townhomes, which were laid out in a semi-circle. He was careful not to block any of the driveways that led into the circle. They were quaint white buildings with brick fronts and dark brown peaked roofs; five buildings in all, each holding two units. He looked at the paper in his hand. The house number was 5669 and was the first driveway to his left.

As he walked up the asphalt drive, Torch could see someone watching him from a bay window in the front. She was holding a cat and petting its fur. The few inches of fresh snow in the yard were crisscrossed with tracks, as if kids had been playing in it. Torch didn't need to ring the bell—she was there at the door before he was.

She was wearing a red sweater with a high neck and black slacks. A gold cross on a chain hung around her neck. She held the cat tight against her bosom and extended her hand, saying, "I'm Doris Malone, won't you please come in."

Torch slipped out of his loafers, and followed Doris as she took him to the back of the house where a small wooden table, with four chairs, looked out over a wedge of backyard. It had a mountain ash tree, still covered with orange berries, as its centerpiece. "Let me take your coat and hat," she said, "and please sit down." She seemed almost overly friendly.

"What a nice cozy home," Torch said. "This is something my wife and I should look into instead of the big house we have."

"I like it," she said, "and the neighborhood is good. Where do you live, detective?"

"Down by Lake Calhoun in Minneapolis," he said. "It's a nice neighborhood but more home than we need."

"Does your wife work?" she asked.

"Yes, she's an attorney."

Torch had placed a yellow legal pad in front on him, and his pen was lying on top of it.

"Can I get you some coffee?" she asked.

"If you have it made, but don't go to any trouble for me." She busied herself behind him for a few minutes, and then came back with a mug of coffee and a small plate of cookies. Then she sat down opposite him, still holding the purring gray cat.

"Doris, when I talked to you on the phone, I mentioned a man named Skip Hendricks and you said you had worked with him in the past. I want you to know I found out that, in the fall of 1992, you had filed charges against Skip and then dropped them. But we'll get back to that subject later. How well did you know Skip, and how long did you work with him?" For a second, Torch detected somewhat of a look of terror on Doris's face.

"Where is Skip Hendricks?" she said.

"In jail," Torch answered. "Hopefully, we can keep him there for a long time."

The last statement seemed to calm Doris down somewhat. She looked as if she was confused and trying to recollect something. She was quiet for a few seconds, and then she said, "Skip and I worked together for about three years. We both drove delivery vans for Flagg's and we shared the same territory so we saw each other a lot."

"What was he like?" Torch asked, sipping his coffee.

"I would say he was a narcissist. Full of himself, and he thought he was quite a ladies man. But in all truthfulness, he turned most women off. We were married for a while."

"I take it he eventually turned you off, too?"

"Not at first, but the more I got to know him, the less I trusted him."

Torch was writing as he spoke. "Why is that?"

"Well, a couple of reasons. But let's get back to what you said when you first sat down, and then you might have your answer."

Torch looked up at her, and there were tears in her eyes. "Are you talking about your filing charges against him?"

"Yes."

"And that was for what?"

"Raping me."

Torch put his pen down as she was crying openly now. He reached across the table and touched her arm. "Why did you drop the charges?" he asked.

"He said he would kill me," she said.

Torch sat back and ran his hands through his hair. There was so much he could tell her right now about Skip, but he better not scare her any more than she already was. *He wanted to tell her that because she didn't go to the police that day, he might have killed others, but maybe later, not now.*

Doris had gotten up and grabbed some Kleenex and was trying to compose herself. She still held on tightly to the cat.

Torch tried to give her some time but she sat back down, composed herself, and started talking.

"Detective, something happened shortly after this incident of him assaulting me, and it may or may not help you, but I want to tell you about it. There was this one address that had a delivery almost every day. It was a beauty shop down on Lake Street. Skip would always take the packages for that address, even if they were in my lot. He asked me for them. You see, we sorted and loaded our own trucks, and they were always parked side by side. Then, one day he asked me to go there instead, and he stopped going to that address anymore."

"Was this before or after he raped you?"

"After," she said."

"Let me get this right. The man raped you, and then told you he would kill you if you told on him, but every day you still worked side by side with him?"

She was crying openly again. "You don't understand. He told me everything had to stay normal, like nothing had happened. I couldn't quit and go someplace else because he said he would find me. I couldn't go to the police because he would kill me, and every day I had to put on this charade like nothing had happened." Her voice was rising, and besides crying, she was getting angry. "Detective, I hated this man more than I ever thought I could ever hate anyone. I wanted to kill him but I didn't have the guts to do it. He ruined my life." She was sobbing again, and the cat jumped down off her lap and went into another room.

Torch wanted to stop the interview. He had put her through too much already. "Just a couple more questions," he said. "Okay?" putting his hand on top of hers. "I know this is hard but you don't know how much you have helped us."

She nodded her head and took a deep breath, biting her lip.

"When did you divorce him?"

"After he was fired from his job and moved away to South Carolina."

"Would you testify against him if we bring charges against him for raping you?"

"And then when he gets off or gets out, he comes and kills me?"

"He's not going to get off or out, I intend to put him away for life."

"How can you be sure?" She asked.

"Trust me…he has bigger problems than raping you."

"What can be worse than that?" she shouted, pounding her fist on the table.

"He has already murdered, Doris. Maybe more than once."

"Who?" she said, calming down.

You give me a few days, and I'll tell you the whole story. Just tell me now that you will testify."

"Okay," she said. Torch went around the table and hugged her. "I feel so bad about what happened to you. Let's make it as right as we can." He put his finger under her quivering chin and lifted her head. "He's not going to hurt anyone again, Doris. Just then the cat jumped onto the table and Torch reached over and picked it up and handed it to her. "This cat is a lucky kitty to have someone like you." He fished in his pocket and gave her his card. Call me anytime you want to talk, or if you think of anything else that would help us. In the meantime, I'll be touch with you. I'll let myself out."

Torch sat in his car looking at his notes. Right now, he knew two things for sure. One was, this guy was going to jail. Two was, somewhere out there was probably an innocent man, who had been found guilty for killing his wife, and he needed to find him now more than ever.

CHAPTER ELEVEN

Barry was so sick he wasn't thinking rationally, and he realized it. It seemed that every day brought another problem. The last few years his life had been primitive and tough, and now all he wanted was to live like other people live, but that's not possible when you're a fugitive. His name was linked to so many databases, be it Social Security or the Department of Motor vehicles. Here he was, 2000 miles away, and yet the eyes of the law were looking for him even here...maybe.

He had told his boss that he was too sick to work right now, and he would be back as soon as he was well. He had a doctor's appointment for tomorrow. The other thing was this afternoon's appointment with the psychiatrist that Father Kevin had arranged for him to see. *How did he talk with this man without revealing who he was, and what he was wanted for? But on the other hand, this was a real opportunity to unlock something from his mind that had haunted him for twenty years.* Sick or not, he was going to keep this appointment.

The appointment with Dr. Bob Holden went better than Barry had imagined. There would be no hypnosis this session, just a "question and answer" session, where Bob would gather information that he could use in the actual session. Bringing back subconscious thoughts needed gentle probing of the mind, and he needed a well thought out plan.

"Father Kevin tells me you have been sick," Bob said, after they had been seated.

"Yes, I have some stomach problems right now. I'm going to see a medical doctor tomorrow."

The room was an inner room with no window, very small, and had only a table and three chairs in it. Barry couldn't help but draw a parallel between it and the police interrogation rooms he had sat in years before.

"I will be recording everything we say here today. It's all confidential and is only for my own use. Is that okay?"

"Yes," Barry answered. *"What choice did he have?"* Last night he had prayed that he was doing the right thing and that God would help the doctor find some answers, but he had to cooperate.

"Barry, I will start by asking you your name."

"Barry Winston." *God, his stomach hurt, and he was getting nauseous again, although he hadn't eaten anything.*

"Tell me about why you're here, and what you hope to accomplish."

Barry fidgeted in the chair. He didn't know where to begin. Finally, he started talking. "I have been accused of doing something I didn't do, and I believe that the identity of the person who did do it is known to me, but I just can't bring it out of my mind."

"What makes you believe this?" Dr. Bob had his eyes closed, and his head tilted back as he talked, as if he was in great thought."

"I guess because I have had recurring dreams about it."

"And you see someone in these dreams?"

"Vaguely, yes."

"Explain 'vaguely.'"

"I see the person, but I don't see the face."

"What is the person doing?"

"Stabbing my wife to death."

"What were you doing while this was going on, and where were you?" Dr. Bob was now taking some notes, too.

"I was right beside her in bed, and too drunk to do anything about it."

"You were unconscious?"

"Yes, for all practical purposes. I was powerless to do anything." *He was going to start retching here in about two minutes.*

"Barry, I want you to describe the scene to me as best you can. Not the actual murder scene as it was happening, but what you saw when you woke up. I know this is hard but I need to know this."

"Can I use the bathroom first?"

"Yes, it's across the hall." He pointed behind him.

Many minutes later, Barry wanted to get up off that cool tile floor, where he had laid his feverish head, and just walk out the front door and go home to his bed, but he knew he had to finish his appointment first. He had the dry heaves, but more than that, for the first time he spit up blood, and that was alarming. Gradually, the waves of nausea that had washed over him seemed to subside and he got to his feet and stood in front of the sink, shivering with weakness. He wadded up some paper towels, wet them down with cold water, and pressed them against his forehead. *Please help me dear Lord,* he prayed. *Give me strength.*

He sat down in the chair, trying to remember where they were in the conversation. Dr. Bob looked up from his notes, saying, "Are you alright?"

"Yes…yes…let's go on," Barry said. "You wanted to know what I saw when I woke up, right? Maybe "becoming conscious" would be a better term. I wasn't asleep."

"That's right, and I agree. Just describe the scene, and then tell me what you told the police when they got there. Do you need a second to collect your thoughts, Barry?"

"No…no," Barry said, almost shouting, "I will never forget what I saw when I woke up. The lights were on and she looked like she was sleeping, except she was covered in blood. She was in her pajamas, and I remember looking down at myself and I was all bloody, too… with her blood!"

"Where was the knife?"

"In my right hand."

"Was your first impression that you had killed her?"

"No. I was still so drunk I couldn't stand up. I remember going to the kitchen to call the police and falling down several times in the hallway."

"Was there a phone in the bedroom?"

"Yes, but I had to get out of there. I thought whoever had done this might still be in the house."

"Were you still dragging the knife around with you?"

"Yes, according to the police I still had it in my hand. I have no memory of that."

"You don't remember it being in your hand when the police arrived?"

"Yes…I mean…no. That's where the police found it, but I do remember waking up with it in my hand."

"Tell me about your recurring dreams where you see someone stabbing her."

Barry appeared to be getting agitated now. He was fidgeting with his hands; twisting his shirttail up in a knot and smoothing it back out. "The dreams are always the same," he said, softly. "I just see the knife going up and down, tearing into her flesh, and she is naked and not resisting…"

"You just said she had her pajamas on when you woke up."

"Yes, someone dressed her."

"Was it you?"

"The police told me I did, but I don't think I was capable of doing it."

"Barry, did you and Kim have a good marriage?"

Barry was staring into his lap. He raised his head and said, "We had a perfect marriage. Can I go now?"

"Yes. I think I have enough for now. When are you going to see a doctor about your health?"

"Tomorrow."

"You look like shit."

"I feel like shit."

"Let me know how you come out. I would like to see you one more time before we try hypnosis. Why don't you call in for an appointment when you feel better."

"Okay," he said, and left the room. Hurrying by the receptionist, he barely made it outside before the retching started again.

Torch and Charlie had just finished supper and he was wiping the dishes as she washed and rinsed them. She was listening to him talk about Skip Henderson. He told Charlie what Doris had told him about the rape.

"You do know that the statute of limitations has passed on charging him with rape? In this state it's nine years."

Torch hadn't thought about that yet, but he knew she was right. "Yes, I know, but I feel that somebody that's programmed like this guy is, hasn't been sitting idle all of these years—that he's done something else we don't know about that is chargeable. I just need to find it."

Charlie said, "There certainly does seem to be a preponderance of evidence that he is a career criminal. You night have to find out more than just what he has done, however. You might have to find Barry Winston, too, and get his side of the story once more."

"We've been trying to find Barry Winston for a long time now but he's disappeared off the map. I'm not sure if he's even alive any more."

"I just feel he might have some answers for you that you haven't thought about. Maybe a fresh look won't hurt. Are you starting to think he might be innocent, Torch?"

"I don't know, Charlie. Had we known about Skip back then, yes, we might have come to another conclusion. New evidence always changes the picture."

"It does seem like Barry was convicted on nothing more than a lot of circumstantial evidence," Charlie said. "I'm not so sure it would fly in today's court."

"So you think your court, today, is better than the courts were then? May I remind you, he was convicted by a jury, not by a judge or the courts."

"No need to get sarcastic, Torch. You have to admit, the burden of proof in cases like this is much higher now." Torch was getting hot under the collar, and was waving his dishtowel around when he talked, so she changed the subject before he broke something.

"I think Doris might be some help to your case, but you are going to have to keep her in the closet."

Torch was now sitting down at the table, deep in thought. *Charlie was right; he had only scratched the surface with Doris. But he was going to have to kick Skip loose because he didn't have enough evidence to hold him or charge him. That could shut Doris up in a hurry if she knew Skip was going free.*

"Let's play some cribbage," he told Charlie, wanting to get off the subject completely. "The winner gets your underwear."

"You can have them right now, Torch. I have another pair," Charlie said, smugly.

Barry was lying in bed with a cold washcloth on his forehead, and Sneaky sitting on his chest. One minute he was burning up, and the next minute he couldn't get warm enough. The little mouse sat up on his haunches, staring at Barry with concern on his little pointed face, and his whiskers twitching. It was a new look he had never seen before from the little creature. His eyes burned, and closing them, he slowly drifted off to sleep.

She came to him as if she had drifted in off a fog bank in the early morning twilight. She had the look of an angel, but the radiance glowing around her seemed to originate from behind her, instead of from within her. It was Kim; there was no mistaking that. His Kim... and she was as whole and as beautiful as he ever remembered her. She wasn't talking; she was just smiling down on him, but somehow he knew she had a message for him, and she was trying to connect on some telepathic connection. She was dressed in white—that was whiter than he had ever seen before. It was a silky fabric that floated in and out as she moved, but yet, Kim didn't really appear angelic in nature.

Barry reached out for her, but the distance between them remained constant, no matter how much he tried to get closer to her. Then she started to get smaller and dimmer, until the void was too great, and she disappeared into the mist.

Then, suddenly, he was there. Was this the man who had killed her? Just as suddenly as he appeared, he was gone, never revealing much more than a shadowy figure holding a knife.

Barry awoke with a start, sitting up in bed, soaking wet with sweat. There was a lump under his hand and when he lifted it from the mattress all he could see were a few drops of blood on the white sheet, and the little gray body of Sneaky. Somehow in his struggles, he had crushed him. He took him in his hand and held his little body to his face and for the first time that Barry could remember, he cried like a baby. It was all too much.

CHAPTER TWELVE

Torch sat in Ray's office at city hall. They had just gone over his conversation with Doris and were talking about their next step.

"I really hate to kick this guy free" Ray said, "But his lawyer is saying, 'charge him or set him free,' and he has a point. It's tough when we know the son-of-a–bitch is probably guilty of enough crimes to keep him in the slammer for the rest of his life. As soon as he gets out of here, we'll probably never find him again."

Torch rubbed his eyes and shook his head slowly. "Charlie and I talked about this for some length last night. What we have on him now isn't going to convict him, but on the other hand, I'm sure there is more out there that we don't know about him. The guy's a cold-blooded killer and they seldom take a vacation for long. I checked today, and the hair shop where Kim worked has been out of business for some time. I called the former owner, who told me that 'One of the girls that Kim was closest with, a gal by the name of Cheryl Cousins, still works around here,' and I would like to bend her ear for a while. She gave me a phone number. She works out at Southtown now. Not in the shopping center, but across the street."

Ray looked puzzled. "How does that tie in with all of this?"

"Well, Doris told me they got packages almost every day, and Skip always wanted to deliver them. He was emphatic about it—even when it wasn't on his route. He had the hots for someone down there, Ray, and I think it was Kim. I just wondered if he talked at all with the other girls, or if they picked up on his interest in Kim. Maybe she had been seeing him, who knows?"

"Was this gone over in the original investigation?" Ray asked.

"No. At the time, her work didn't seem to have any ties connecting it to what happened that night. I don't recall talking to anyone she worked for."

"Tell me again why her husband seemed so guilty back then."

"Well, he was arrested that night because he had her blood all over him. His prints were the only ones on the knife. He had no alibi except to say he was passed out drunk when it happened. There was no sign of a break-in. We had everything, except a good motive, for him to have done it. He also had a lousy lawyer that, from the start, wanted him to take a plea. When Barry wouldn't do it, he gave him a half-hearted attempt of a defense." Torch had talked so fast, spitting all of that out, he had to stop and catch his breath.

"So tell me now why you think he might not have done it. Nothing has changed except for the DNA evidence that says Skip might have been there."

"Right now, Ray, I'm not sure what I think. I wish I had Barry to talk to again. His fifteen years on the run which, by the way, I took as another sign of guilt, doesn't seem that way to me anymore. Let's turn Skip loose, and see if we can get the judge to agree to set some constraints on his whereabouts so we can find him again, and let's see if I can find a smoking gun somewhere."

"That seldom works, Torch, but I'll try."

"In the meantime, I'm going to talk to this other beautician and with Doris again. I have a feeling that Doris left out a few things. I would also like to take a trip to South Carolina to talk to the men who charged him down there, and find out why they had to set him free. I hear the Carolina's are nice this time of the year."

Ray pointed to the door as his phone rang.

When Barry was done crying he tried to get back up off the bed, but for some reason, his legs wouldn't hold him and he collapsed back into the bed. The room seemed to be spinning and growing smaller. He had to vomit again, and this time it was all blood. He managed to dial 911, and then collapsed while sliding out of the bed and onto the floor.

He was aware of hands under him, and bright lights above him that made him squint, and a nurse saying excitedly "B.P. 77 over 35." Then, mercifully, he passed out again.

When he woke up, he was in a hospital bed with tubes in both of his arms; a shadowy figure was moving around at the head of his bed.

The man was elderly, wearing a doctor's coat, with his stethoscope hanging over his shoulder. He was feeling along Barry's collarbone, with his fingers, as he spoke.

"Welcome back. What's your name?" he asked.

"Barry," was all he could mutter.

"Well, Barry, you are a very sick man right now. I'm not sure what all is wrong with you but we are going to get to the bottom of it. We gave you three units of blood, and will be running some tests in a couple of hours to find out what is going on with you. How long have you been sick?"

"A few weeks." His eyes were focusing better now, and he could make out a nurse, who was on the other side of the bed.

"To start with, let's get him down to x-ray for a scan of his belly and then do a complete blood workup. Keep him on the IV and for now, no food or water by mouth."

The nurse nodded her head. She looked young and pretty and very compassionate. "Barry, is there someone we could call? Family or friends? By the way, my name is Audrey, and if you need anything, push the button on this remote and someone will be right here."

"I would like to talk with Father Kevin if I could."

"You can do that...he's here almost every day. I'll see he gets the message. I'm going to give you something to relax you, and then someone will come and get you for tests. Okay?"

Barry nodded his head as she injected something into the tube in his arm. "You just relax now."

Audrey Snyder had worked at the Fairbanks hospital for ten years now, and all of it in Intensive Care. She'd seen almost very kind of injury and illness that existed. Audrey had helped bring people back from the dead, and she had been there holding their hands when they breathed the last breath of air that would ever enter their bodies. Tears had slid down her cheeks and fallen on the floor, more times than she wanted to remember, for the people she had helped. But experience told her, that in order to survive as a good nurse, hanging on to those memories would only take away from her ability to help her patients.

Right now though, this man was as sick as she remembered any patient being for some time. He seemed different from the run-of-the-mill homeless and indigenous people that so often came through the doors here. Most of the people who didn't fit into that category usually had loved ones or friends that would accompany them, but this man seemed so alone in the world. Audrey looked at her watch. She was off in fifteen minutes. Her daughter would be home from school in a few minutes, and although she was ten now, she didn't like to leave her alone any longer than she had to. "Fight hard, my friend," she whispered, brushing the hair from his eyes. *His fever was still raging* she thought, feeling his forehead. Just then, the doors banged open and they were there with a gurney to take him to Radiology.

Torch was on the phone, trying to find a time when he could talk with Cheryl Cousins, and she wasn't being very helpful.

"Kim Winston," she said, in a southern drawl. "My God man, that child has been gone how long and you want to talk about it some more?"

"It's important," Torch said, "or I wouldn't be bothering you."

"Well, I get home at three, and I guess I can give you a few minutes. Any chance you could fix some parking tickets for me?" She chuckled.

Torch laughed, too. "Today at three…okay?"

"Yeah, okay, but just for a few minutes."

"What's your address?"

"The building's called the *Conway on East Eighteenth*—just buzz me from the lobby and I'll let you in."

Torch remembered the Conway as an upper crust building in its day that had fallen on bad times, and now was a haven for druggies and prostitutes. *Oh well, don't judge a book by its cover,* he thought. His phone rang.

"Torch, its Ray." We had to kick Skip loose. He has to check in with a probation officer once a week and stay in the area. I only got that because he has some misdemeanor crap from years ago staring him in the face, that he never took care of. It's enough to keep him close, but not for long. The judge gave him a court date of February

16th. If he doesn't get jail time out of those charges, and I doubt he will, after that he will be free to go wherever he wants.

"Bastard," said Torch, and hung up thinking, *who the hell talked me into getting involved in this shit again?*

The next morning, Father Kevin looked at the note in his hand, given to him by his secretary, Darla. It simply said, "Stop by and see Barry Winston in I.C.U at Fairbanks General. He has asked for you." He looked on the backside of the note, but there was nothing more. *I wonder what this is all about,* he thought. *I know he hasn't felt good for some time.* He had just seen Doctor Bob at the clinic this morning, and the doctor had remarked about their conversation, and mentioned that Barry didn't look good physically. *Maybe he would go over now,* he thought.

"I'm going over to the hospital," he told Darla, and he was out the door.

Barry was propped up in bed and feeling better. He still had a lot of tubes attached, and he wasn't able to get out of bed, even if he wanted to. The nurse, Audrey, had been in and told him his test results were back and one of the doctors would be in shortly to discuss the results with him.

"Can I have something to drink?" he asked, his eyes pleading like a Lab puppy at the supper table.

"I can give you some ice chips to suck on for now. How would that be? Let's see what the doctor says when he gets here, and maybe we can do better." She smiled and patted his hand. All Barry could think was, *as sick as he was, she looked beautiful to him—and was so nice.*

Just then, two doctors walked in, looking very somber. The taller of the two, a very distinguished-looking man, said to Barry, "How long have you been sick, my friend?" By the way, I'm Doctor Erickson, Chief of surgery here and this is Doctor Peal, who is a doctor of internal medicine, and oncology," he added.

"Nice to meet both of you," Barry said. "To answer your question, I've been feeling sick for a few weeks."

The surgeon let out a sigh and said, "Barry, you have some serious liver problems. I won't know for sure until we get a biopsy, but you might have liver cancer. In fact, I would miss my bet if you don't have it."

"What does that mean?" Barry asked. "I'm going to die?"

"Well, let's talk about that after we get the biopsy, but if it is cancer, it's serious."

"Dr. Peal can talk more about treatment programs with you then. You're a fairly young man, so we would like to get as aggressive as we can be in treating it—if that, indeed, is what it is. I have you scheduled to go down to surgery this afternoon and we will do a little exploratory surgery. I just need your permission." He had a clipboard and a pen, which he laid on the bed.

Barry picked it up and read the consent form, then signed it and handed it back to him.

"Any other questions?" Doctor Erickson asked.

Barry shook his head and both doctors left. He could see them through the window into the hallway having, what looked like, a serious conversation with the nurse, Audrey. She looked extremely concerned. Just then, Father Kevin walked in.

CHAPTER THIRTEEN

Torch parked in front of the Conway in a cab zone and flipped his car's visor down, where he had put the police I.D. that Ray had given him, showing that he was on official police business. He brought his pad and pen along and walked up the gray cement steps into the lobby, which was decorated for Christmas. Looking at the mailbox rack, he found C. Cousins and pushed the buzzer under the name.

She was a large black woman with flawless features. Her neck was strung with many necklaces, and her wrists were similarly adorned. She gave Torch a big toothy smile and said, "Come on in…I got half an hour. After that, you're on your own."

The apartment was sparsely furnished but had been done with good taste. She motioned him to a chair in the living room, and then sat at his right in a matching chair. "I could make you some coffee if you would like, but I don't have much to eat."

"No, that's fine," Torch said. "I just have a few questions. You do remember Kim Winston?"

"Yes, we worked together many years. She was one of my best friends until her husband killed her."

Torch let that remark pass, but asked her if she also remembered a courier from a package company named Flagg's. "His name was Skip Henderson," Torch remarked. He fished in his pocket and brought out a mug shot of Skip, taken just the other day. "He would have been about twenty years younger than in this picture," he said.

She looked at the photo for some time and then handed it back to him. "Yeah, I remember him alright. Kim was terrified of him."

"Why so?" Torch asked.

"Because he was always making suggestive remarks to her. It got so she would go in the back when she saw him coming down the sidewalk."

"What kind of suggestive remarks?" Torch asked.

"Oh, he was always talking about what a man he was, and how happy she would be if she would have dumped Barry and came and lived with him. Guess it turns out Barry was no prize either, huh? Poor girl, she deserved better than that scum."

"Did she ever cut Skip's hair, or is there any way she would have come in contact with some of Skip's hair?"

"No way! The dude always kept his cap on and she wouldn't go near him. I have no idea who cut his hair, but it wasn't in our shop. We never cut men's hair. Why all the interest in this guy all of a sudden?"

"Well, I can't say yet, but he's in some trouble, and we're just trying to connect some dots. Look, I would like to talk to you again sometime, but for now, my half hour is up and I have to run and get out of your hair. No pun intended," he said, with a smile.

"Well, I hope you find what you're looking for," she said.

"I hope so, too," Torch said, and handed her his card. "Call me if you think of anything else."

Torch walked down the hallway to the steps, and he was on the next landing when Cheryl caught up with him. "Wait," she said. "I do have something else. Skip assaulted Kim one day when she was alone in the shop. She swore me to secrecy. Told me he would kill us both if we told anyone."

"Do you mean he raped her?"

"I'm not sure, but yes, I think he might have. Kim wouldn't get specific about it, and got mad if we pressed her for more information."

They waited a second for another person to get by them and out the door. "When Barry was on trial, why didn't you come forward with that information?" Torch asked.

Cheryl was crying now. "I thought he would kill me," she sobbed.

"Did you not think he could have been the one who killed Kim?"

"Yes, that entered my mind, but you guys seemed like you had such a strong case against her husband." She paused to wipe her face. "Did he kill her and is he still on the loose?" She asked.

Torch took back his handkerchief he had given her and stuffed it in his back pocket. "I'm not sure, and yes, he is on the loose. But you have nothing to worry about. He doesn't know I'm talking to you. Look, I'm sorry to upset you. Please call me for any reason." He patted her hand and then gave her a one-shoulder hug. "Thank you for being so brave," he said.

Back in the car and driving away, Torch pounded on the steering wheel so hard he nearly ran into some parked cars. He was not only angry because it appeared they might have convicted the wrong man, he was angry that now he probably had the right man and couldn't do anything about it; and he had no idea where Barry was so that he could make it right.

Father Kevin sat beside Barry's bed. The anesthesia they had given him was still affecting him and he was sleeping comfortably. The verdict had been short and painful. Barry's liver and two other organs were full of cancer. They would start treatment tomorrow, but the outlook was not good.

The young priest had a small book of prayers in his hands, and he recited them softly, but audibly. Barry had come back to the Lord and now, more than any other time, he needed God back in his life. Father was just the go-between.

His thoughts strayed to the things Barry had told him in confidence—that he was an accused and convicted, but innocent, murderer. He remembered Barry talking about wanting revenge and wanting to kill the detective who had wrongly accused him and ruined his life. *There was a far better way to resolve this,* Father thought. *Help the law catch the real guilty person.*

But now this, and he had no idea how long Barry had left, or how to help him. His prayer turned from one of healing, to one of understanding how to help Barry.

Audrey and another nurse came back into the room and checked his bandages. The other nurse left and Audrey stood by the end of the bed, her eyes welling with tears. She, too, knew the score, but right now she needed God, also. Father Kevin reached over and touched her hand, and they prayed together.

Skip Hendricks stood on the courthouse steps, waiting for the cab that would take him to his friend's house. He would play their game for now, and abide by the rules. While he'd been in jail he wondered what evidence they really had on him. They had kept most of it close to their breast. He did know that this was some kind of evidence from the scene of the killing of Kim—something that tied him to the scene. The detective had mentioned him working for Flagg's. Was there someone there who, after all these years, was making trouble for him? He thought long and hard. Then the name popped into his head. *Doris Malone. How many years had he and that bitch been together and worked together? Did she still work for Flagg's? Yes, she could have known something. She was always asking questions about why he wanted the packages for the shop where Kim worked. Accusing him of having a thing for Kim. He never could figure out why she hadn't said something at Barry's trial. He should have got rid of her when he had a chance, but man, it's been twenty years and how the hell would they find her after twenty years? Well, if they could find her, he could too.*

The black Range Rover pulled up to the curb, and the window lowered. "Skip—get in the car, dude," the driver said.

Barry started his chemo the next day. He would be in the hospital for the rest of the week and then, the day before Christmas, he was getting out. His treatments would go on for weeks on an outpatient basis.

Audrey came to see him several times a week, and sometimes twice a day. She held his shoulders when he was racked with nausea, and spent hours in the bathroom fighting waves of throwing up. She washed out his mouth, and brushed his teeth, after the vomiting left him utterly exhausted. She changed his wet gown when he was soaked from sweating, and brought him extra warm blankets when he fought the chills. She took his hand and walked down the hall and back, trying to help him get his strength back so he could leave on Friday. He seemed to be her favorite patient.

On Friday morning, Audrey gathered all of Barry's things and wheeled him down to the lobby. They seemed to have his nausea under control for the time being, and he had some breakfast under his belt even though he had no appetite. Father Kevin was there with his Jeep to give him a ride home.

As she let the footpads on the wheelchair down, and helped Barry up, Audrey gave him a slip of paper. "Barry, this is my home number.

I want to help you get through this so please call me when you are settled. Call me if you just want to talk, or wonder about symptoms you might be having. I want you to be my special project."

She reached up and kissed him on the cheek. Barry's eyes were filling with tears. He wasn't used to having people care about him like this. "Thank you," he croaked and reached out and touched her cheek.

"I want to thank you for the ride and all of the prayers and attention you have given me," Barry said to Father Kevin.

"It's the least I can do," the priest said. "That pretty little nurse seems to want to make sure your body gets healed, and I still want to work on getting your soul back where it belongs."

Barry laughed. "She is pretty, isn't she?"

Father gave him a playful punch in the shoulder.

Torch was worried because he had created a conundrum of sorts. Skip probably knew he had talked to Doris, and Skip also probably knew where Doris lived. *But Skip also knew he was being watched,* Torch thought. *But on the other hand, this was no rational man. He had broken so many laws, so many times, always staying one step ahead of the law. He knew how to play the game and he played it well.*

Torch was waiting for him to make that fateful mistake all crooks make, sooner or later, but Doris couldn't be left as a pawn in the game. Now he was on his way over to her house for a strategy session, and this wasn't going to be easy. He had promised her he would keep her safe and not involve her, and he had already reneged on part of that. He had to be careful, because right now she was his star witness.

The last time he was here Doris had been all dressed up, but this morning she looked like death warmed over. She had on an old gray sweatshirt and some faded blue jeans with holes in the knees. "Come in," she said, looking over his shoulder and outside as if to make sure he was alone.

"I won't be long," Torch said. "I just wanted you to know that Skip has been let loose. Nothing we have said or done should lead him to you, but you never know what this type of person is thinking!"

"Loose," she said, her eyes showing concern. "Couldn't you at least charge him with raping me?"

"The statute of limitations has run out on that one." Torch was fingering his hat, and having a hard time making eye contact with

Doris. "I wish we could. He's guilty of a lot of things, Doris, but putting them all together into a case a jury will buy takes time."

"Twenty years isn't enough time," she shouted.

Torch was getting more uneasy. "Look, Doris, I don't make the laws; I just try to enforce them. Had your rape been reported in a timely manner, he would still be in jail. Now that being said, I know why you didn't report it, and I'm not trying to blame you. Work with me here and we'll still convict him. I would like to talk to you some more about Skip, but not today. I want you to think long and hard about that time in your life, and if there was anything you think might tie him to Kim's death. Tomorrow is Christmas Eve day and I want you to enjoy your holiday. After Christmas, I'll get back to you, okay?"

"Okay," she said.

"Keep your doors locked, and if you see anybody that looks like Skip, call the police immediately. You've got my number so call me if you want to talk, or if you have anything you think we can use. Chances are, after all these years, this man isn't even thinking about you," Torch said. Putting his arm around her shoulders, he gave her a little hug and she responded with a weak smile.

As he walked back to his car, he felt tired. The same tired he used to feel before he retired. It had been foolish for him to get involved in this again, but done was done, and he was going to see it through. For now, he was going home, but first he had to go find a Christmas gift for Charlie. He sat back in the seat and lit a cigarette. *What in the hell was he going to get her?*

CHAPTER FOURTEEN

Winters are hard in Alaska, and Fairbanks was in the thick of a numbing cold spell. Last night, the temperature had dipped to forty below. The rivers had frozen over and so had the windows in his cheap apartment. Tomorrow was Christmas Eve, and although better than the ones he had experienced in the wilderness, life wasn't looking too rosy for Barry.

He had a slight fever yet, but otherwise felt a lot better. No real bad effects from the chemo…yet! His next appointment wasn't until Tuesday—the day after Christmas.

His rent was due next week, and Barry had only a few dollars left in his pocket. This afternoon he was going down to the office to talk to them about an extension. If that wasn't possible, he didn't know what he was going to do. Right now, there was a knock on the door.

She looked so different out of uniform that he hardly recognized her. "Hi, Barry. How goes the battle?"

"Audrey? What…how…?"

"It's my day off, silly, and I was worried about you so I thought I would stop by and see how you are feeling. You're not busy, are you?"

"No…no…not at all, come on in."

She had some soup in a thermos, and she washed them a couple of cups and sat down by the small table. Seeing the cage on the table she asked, "Do you have a bird?" she asked.

Barry blushed. "No, it was a mouse that I kept for a pet. It died and it's part of a long story. Foolish, huh?"

"Not at all," Audrey said, pouring them both some soup. "Tell me about yourself, Barry. You don't sound like you're a native."

"Well, I have lived here for over five years. But for four of them, I had no one to talk to."

"Why is that?" she asked, quizzically.

"Because I was living in the wilderness. This soup is delicious," Barry said.

"Thank you. You know you have to eat well or your treatments are going to be very hard on you."

Barry was quiet for a moment, and then he said, softly, "Audrey, am I going to die?"

She smiled, and reaching across the table, touched his hand. "Not if I can help it," she said. "Now tell me why you were living in the wilderness. Prospector?"

For the next half hour Barry poured out his life story while Audrey listened intently. There was no sense in keeping any secrets anymore.

She was sitting back in her chair, with her arms folded across her chest. Her eyes were welling with tears, but she made no attempt to wipe them away. "Your life has been hard, Barry. I can't imagine going through what you've been through. Let me help you fight this battle."

Barry was overcome now, too. *Why was she being so nice to him? Was this something inherent to nurses or did she really care.* "Audrey, I'm not sure why you want to help someone with all of my baggage, but I'm touched by your kindness."

"Hush and roll up your sleeve. I want to take your temp and blood pressure before I go." She felt around in the bottom of the bag for her stethoscope and cuff. "For now," she said, "let's keep this our secret. I don't want to get in trouble at work. No fraternizing, they say, with the patients."

"Mums the word," he said.

Audrey spent a few minutes cleaning up the place, and then told Barry that she had to leave. "I'll see you on Tuesday, my friend. Merry Christmas!"

"Merry Christmas, Audrey, and thank you so much." He needed to rest for a while, and then go see the landlord about his rent.

Skip was nursing a bad headache from all of the drugs he had done last night. Skip was not a good person and he knew it, but there was no shame in him for what he had done, and less shame for what he was contemplating. He was a shrewd criminal who had learned to play the justice system for all of its weaknesses, and so far, it had worked well for him.

However, something was bothering him right now. *Why, after all of these years, after the death of Kim, was this case being fired back up again?* He hadn't been involved in the original trial; in fact, he hadn't even been accused or thought of. The cops had latched onto an innocent man, who couldn't defend himself, and he had been the benefactor of that snafu. Now, however, they seemed to think maybe they had erred…but why? What was the smoking gun here, and was her name Doris? He intended to find out, but it could wait until after the holidays.

Father Kevin was kneeling on the steps in front of the altar. Mass was over, and the people had left, but he was troubled about Barry Winston's case, and now he was asking his Lord to give him guidance. He knew of Barry's troubles with the law, back in Minnesota, and although he tended to believe Barry when he said he was innocent, he had no proof of that. He wanted to help him prove his innocence, but he wasn't sure if he was doing things that were not really in his job description as a Catholic Priest. He had a plan of action, and right now, he was just asking for guidance.

On the other hand, he was well aware that Barry was probably not going to be able to overcome this latest attack on him, the cancer that had progressed so far along before he went in for treatment. *Was there even time to defend Barry before the malignant cells took his life?* He strongly believed that every person deserved their day in court, and he wasn't talking about God's court, he was talking about man's court. It was one thing to be accused of something and be innocent, but it was another thing to die being accused when you were innocent and going to your grave, seemingly in the public's eye, a guilty man.

It was so easy when dealing with God's laws because God was all-knowing and there was no hiding the truth from him. You were either innocent or you weren't. But Father Kevin wasn't God and he didn't have his insight so now, here he was, asking for that direction. He was also asking for God's healing power for Barry, but wasn't sure if that was possible, either. His faith was being tested.

Barry had come to him last night. His apartment manager was not willing to help him with his rent. "I want to come back and stay with you here for just a few days until I get stronger and can go back to work."

Father Kevin was young but in some ways he was old beyond his years. "Barry, you are too sick to live here. We have people come in here every day, with God knows what, when it comes to communicable illnesses. You can't risk that."

Barry was quiet for a moment, and then Father said. "I'm going to talk with some social services people to see if I can get you some help. In the meantime, the church will help you with your rent."

"How will I ever repay you?" Barry asked.

"It's not me you need to thank Barry, its God."

Christmas Day dawned cold and dark in the Yukon and in Fairbanks. Yesterday, when the sun did shine, it didn't seem to warm up that much. If you looked closely, you could see the sundogs alongside it. You only saw them when it was extremely cold. Barry was deeply depressed, with a seemingly incurable disease, and feeling all alone in this cold world. *How could things get much worse?*

Around three in the afternoon there was a knock on the door, and it was Audrey. She was on her way home from work and had stopped to see him. She hugged him for a lingering moment and then, going to the table, she unwrapped a turkey dinner she had smuggled out of the hospital commissary. Slipping out of her coat, she said, "Come eat before it gets any colder." She also brought coffee and some chocolate cream pie for both of them.

Barry reached for the pie, and she slapped his fingers, "Not until you eat your dinner, Barry."

"Why are you being so nice to me?" he said, with a quizzical look on his face.

"Because I like you, Barry."

"You do know I'm going to die?"

"We're all going to die someday Barry, some of us sooner than others. I looked at your last tests and you are doing great. People have beaten this disease for a long time, Barry. You have to be positive.'"

He stared at her for a while. She was beautiful in her own little way. So petite and delicate-looking, with dark black eyes that seemed to be wet all the time. They reminded him of the lava glass rocks he had found once, in a mountain stream. Her face, framed by that jet-black hair cut short in a Dutch boy style, fit her little body to a tee and seemed to be always smiling, as if she was up to something. She was one of the few positive things in Barry's negative world. The attention was comforting, but at the same time, he wondered, "*Why?*"

She stared back at him and reaching across the table, touched the top of his hand with her fingertips. Her hands, like the rest of her, were so delicate and warm to the touch. "We are going to get you well, Barry. You just wait and see."

After they were done eating, Barry went to lie down for a while. He still had some nausea problems and wanted to keep his Christmas dinner down. Audrey sat on the side of the bed, holding his hand. "You need a haircut," she said. "Maybe tomorrow I'll bring a scissors along and see what I can do."

Barry smiled weakly. "Why are you being so nice to me?" he asked again.

"Why are you asking?" she answered. "You got too many friends already?"

"No," he said. "I just have nothing to offer you but work and heartaches."

"You let me worry about that."

Torch was worried that Skip might try to connect some dots and dashes and go after Doris; but if he told her that, he would just make things worse after he had told her 'not to worry.' *Why did we have to have a legal system that was more concerned about the crooks rights than the victims, and how many times had he asked that question in his years of police work?* The second question going through his mind was *why was he getting involved in it at all when he had turned in his badge?* Something wouldn't let him let go of this case. The initial conversation with Doris hadn't gone well and he knew it. Torch slammed his hand down on the tabletop, spilling his coffee. Damn this system, and damn the attorneys, and damn everything. It was time to take Charlie out for a nice supper, and to put this crap on the back burner for a while.

They went to a Chinese place downtown and had sweet and sour chicken, and spicy rice. Charlie seemed to be happy to be able spend some time with her husband. Lately, they had been going in different directions way too often.

"How's your workload?" Torch asked.

"About the same. Next week we have preliminary hearings on the Gussimer case. You remember that one—it happened before you retired."

"Was that the asshole that shot up the school lunchroom because he was pissed about having to be there?"

"You do remember."

"His dad hired a very good attorney for him. It won't be easy. They want him tried as a juvenile, but I know this judge and I'm not sure he will allow that. Hope not, anyway."

"Wasn't he eighteen?"

"Not until a couple of weeks after his shooting spree."

"Damn, this chicken is good, Charlie. How did you hear about this place?" Torch had had enough talk about courtrooms and judges.

"It's always been here."

"You just got hung up on that blond waitress over at Whitey's and refused to go anywhere else."

"You mean Wendy?" Torch said, with a smile. "She did have a nice rack, but I bet if you took her bra off they would hang to the floor."

"I wouldn't know about such things, Torch. How's your case working out?"

"Horse shit. I haven't enough evidence to arrest this jerk yet, and now he knows about one of my witnesses. I'm worried he might try to get in touch with her."

"How are you going to protect her?"

"I have to go see Ray in the morning to see if I can get someone assigned to her. If not, I might have to stake out her place myself."

"Sounds serious."

"It is. Want some more wine?"

"Are you trying to get me drunk?"

"Yeah. Do you have any objections, counselor?"

"Not if you stay home tonight and take care of business."

Torch held up two fingers to get the waiter's attention. "More wine," he said.

CHAPTER FIFTEEN

On Sunday afternoon, Father Kevin came to see Barry. The two men sat side by side on the edge of the bed. Father brought him communion, and they prayed for God's grace, and a good outcome for Barry's cancer.

"I've been thinking about the pickle you're in, back in Minnesota," Father said. "You need to try and get it cleared up."

"If I go back there, I'm going to be arrested, no matter what I say, Father. Besides, I can't go anywhere right now with my ongoing treatments."

"I'm not suggesting you go back right now, I just want you to get this thing off your conscience. I believe you're innocent, and you need to go back to Dr. Bob and see if he can help you with this. I saw him this morning after Mass, and he asked about you."

Barry had almost forgotten about his meeting with the psychiatrist and hypnotist. "When does he want to see me?" he said. "It all seems so futile right now, with this cancer eating away at me."

"You're not dead yet, Barry," Father said, squeezing his shoulder. "God will make it right with your body. You need to make this thing right with your mind."

They talked some more about his debt to the church, and Barry said, "I am going to repay every dime, Father—as soon as I'm well enough to go back to work."

"I'm not worried about it, Barry." Then, changing the subject he said, "How's Audrey?"

Barry was somewhat startled by the question. *How did he know about her?* "She's fine," he stammered. "I'm not sure why she has such an interest in me, but I'm grateful."

Father had gotten up and walked across the room, and was looking out the frost-covered window. "You're not just a patient to her, Barry. I hope you realize that." He had turned, and was looking over his shoulder as he talked. "How do I know that, my friend? Let's just say she is one of my patients." He walked over and picked up his coat from the chair where he had left it. "Call Dr. Bob and make an appointment. Pray for healing, and not just for your body. See you in Mass on Sunday. You need to get out, anyway."

Barry walked him to the door and the two men hugged. "Thanks, Father, for coming."

Father Kevin smiled, but said nothing else as he stepped out into the cold Fairbanks air. He couldn't get any more involved in Barry's case than he already was, but he could point him in the right direction.

His appointment with Dr. Bob was Thursday morning, and Father Kevin came over and gave him a ride to the office. "I'll be back in a couple of hours to pick you up," he said, "but call if you get done early."

He remembered the last time he was here—lying on the floor in the bathroom, puking, and wondering what in the hell was the matter with him. Today, although weak, he felt fine and was anxious to get this over with, anxious to get at the truth if it was there.

The receptionist asked him to take a seat, as the doctor was still with a patient. She was young, and although seemingly busy, Barry caught her looking his way more than once. *Was she trying to figure out why he was here, or was she truly interested in him and his welfare?*

The office was very simple, with a few pictures of local wildlife and the good doctor's credentials hanging on the wall for everyone to see. Graduated from Purdue University in Indiana. Awarded all of the privileges and freedoms to practice the medicine of looking into troubled minds. *How many stories had he heard in his years of practice? Like Father Kevin, he was privy to what was on people's minds and what was troubling them. His way was to try and heal them, while Father's way was to try and get forgiveness for them for any wrongs they had done.*

The phone rang, and the pretty receptionist turned from her computer to answer it. She quickly transferred the call to some unknown location, smiling softly at Barry as she caught him looking her way. His years on the run and in the wild left him clumsy, at best, when it came to conversing with the opposite sex. Then the door opened, and there he was. Not in a white coat or a suit, but in blue jeans and a green cardigan sweater. "Barry, come in," he said, offering his hand. "I understand you've been sick and in treatment. How's that going?"

"Okay, I guess. Not sure just what is going on, but they tell me I'm getting better."

"I have a couch like all psychiatrists have for their patients, but for now, I prefer that we both sit on it, and talk for a while. I need to know what it is that you are looking for. I know you're having problems that need to be resolved. Father Kevin told me a little about it, so first, I need to get to know more about you. Then we need to figure out what it is that we are looking for, and how to get there."

"Do you think the answers are there, Doc?"

"We can't ever be sure, Barry, until we try. You'd be surprised what your subconscious mind can hide on you—right there under your nose."

Audrey had washed out Sarah's long blonde hair and chased her off to bed. She had school in the morning, and every night was a fight to get her to settle down. She was an energetic ten years old, with a little bit of an independent mind, but they had a good mother daughter relationship. She knew, in a few years when Sarah was older, it might be more trying. Being a single mother wasn't easy and her apartment, although small, was comfortable. For just the two of them, it was sufficient.

Sarah's father had left to go hunting one day, seven years ago, and he never came back. They found his truck parked alongside a swollen river that was half covered in ice. They theorized that he was trying to wash up after gutting a deer, and may have slipped and fallen in. No body was ever found. It had been seven long years now and she was past grieving. The marriage was not one you would call "made in heaven" to start with, but they did get along. There weren't a lot of men to be had here in the Yukon, and she had felt lucky to have found one.

For now, she was relaxing in the tub and trying to sort out her feelings for this reticent and sick man she had become infatuated with. Maybe, at first, it was pity that brought him to her attention, but over the last few weeks it was more than compassion and she knew it. She enjoyed seeing him and tending to his illness, and the treatments, at first, were the bridge she needed to get close to him. Now however, it was getting to be less of an excuse as he fast approached remission, and she needed to find a new reason to stay close to him. The time was coming when that would no longer be a valid reason for her to go to him. She had to be careful, as the hospital had strict rules about fraternizing with patients. She could lose her job. Somehow, she needed to let him know she cared for him more than he was aware of, and to find out if he cared for her, too. She slid down in the warm water and closed her eyes. Tomorrow she was going to light the flame and see if he wanted to burn it with her. There was the chance he wouldn't survive his cancer, but for now she didn't care. She crossed her arms across her breasts and pretended it was Barry holding her.

Doctor Bob was intent on listening to every word Barry had to say. In a way, this was new ground for him and he knew the ramifications; that it could draw him into a criminal investigation and he didn't want that if he could avoid it. But he felt that the recurring dreams Barry had experienced meant something, and maybe he could help. Barry had walked him through the whole scenario—from the night of the murder to the present day—and how he knew that he was innocent.

"Do the dreams vary or are they all the same?" he asked, after Barry told him about them.

"No, they're pretty much the same. It seems like the answers are there someplace, I just can't get at them. It's like there is a wall that I need to get around."

"Well, I'm not sure if they're there or not, Barry, but it's worth a try. I would say we need to video tape this session if you want to use it for legal purposes. I would also like to administer a drug to you that will help your mind relax. As sick as you have been, are you sure that the ends are going to justify the means here?"

"What do you mean?" Barry asked.

"Has your oncologist given you any progress reports on your long-term prognosis?"

"You mean, am I going to live to see this through?"

"Yes…I'm sorry, that's being blunt of me, but I had to say it."

"You know, doctor, even if I don't survive I want to die a free man. That's important to me. Can you understand that?"

"Yes, I can. I'm sorry, but I had to ask the question. Let's move on. I am going to give you another appointment for next week, and then I will be set up to go through the whole routine. I want you to know, Barry, this is kind of a shot in the dark right now. I know you want the answers. Let's hope they are there."

It was Wednesday morning and Torch and Ray were meeting at the police station. Ray was disturbed about the route this investigation was taking. He was looking out the window at the traffic on the street below as he talked to Torch, who was sitting across from his desk. Torch had asked him for advice on how to protect Doris.

"You know, Torch, in every investigation we involve innocent people. We do our best not to get them in trouble with the accused, but sometimes, the word gets out and there is nothing we can do about it. I firmly believe that Skip would not be foolish enough to approach Doris. That would give us the reason we need to lock him up, and he knows it." Ray had turned around and was now sitting down behind his desk. He was looking into his coffee cup as if it he was reading tea leaves. "We owe it to Doris to tell her that he is out there, and if he tries to contact her, she should call us."

"I agree with you," Torch said. "I just wanted to get your take on it. I really wish that we could get our hands on Barry because I think the answers lie with him."

"We've done our best to catch him, but you know yourself, if someone is smart enough and crafty enough, they can be hard to find, and harder yet to bring in. I guess I could issue a fresh warrant on him. It's been years since most people even thought about him."
"Not for me, it hasn't." Torch muttered. "Not for me."

Audrey was taking a chance with her job—seeing Barry again—but right now she was obsessed with him and didn't care. They could tell her how to nurse, but they weren't going to tell her how to love. Today, she was going to tell Barry she had feelings for him that went beyond medical reasons. She had put on a nice skirt and a frilly white blouse, and just a dab of perfume and lipstick. He had never seen her in anything but hospital garb, without makeup, so she wondered what his thoughts would be when he saw her. She had spent the morning making him some beef stew and fresh baked bread, which also was a change from hospital food. Gathering everything up in a little box, she looked around the room once more to see if she had forgotten anything. *Just some courage to say what she had to say,* she thought. She felt the lock click behind her as she stepped out into the cold. It was just a couple of miles to Barry's place.

Barry was sitting at the table, just looking out the window when she knocked. Life had been such a roller coaster lately that he didn't know what to think any more. Sometimes, he wondered if the struggle was worth it. But he had those same thoughts back in the forest in that log cabin many times, and things weren't that bad now. *Yes, he had cancer,* he thought *but so far, the tests were positive and he didn't really care about living to ninety. He just wanted to live long enough to avenge his wife's death and then whoever wanted him could have him.* He was finally feeling like himself again, and the doctors had told him he could go back to work as soon as he got his strength back. The tumors had been reduced to just a small shadow on the X-rays, and there was hope they would disappear even more. "You never know with cancer," they had told him. "You hope and pray for the best, and sometimes it works out, and sometimes it doesn't." Barry's body had been very receptive to the chemo.

She knocked lightly, and when he opened the door, he was surprised and confused to see her dressed as she was. He could smell her perfume and the look on her face was something new to him. She had always been so professional and every bit the nurse.

"Can I come in?" she asked impishly.

"Audrey. Yes…I…I have never seen you dressed up like this," he stammered. "You look so nice."

"Barry, we need to talk," she said, still smiling, "and thank you."

"What about?" he asked.

"Us," she said. "Can I sit down?"

Barry brought the coffee pot to the table as she sat down across from him. "I have some old doughnuts," he said.

Audrey smiled and said, "Just coffee."

"Barry, I can't see you anymore, as a nurse."

He looked up at her with a puzzled look on his face, but said nothing.

"But," she said, "I can see you as your friend. Does that make sense to you?"

For Barry, a light bulb had been lit, and he was suddenly aware of what Audrey was saying. Now it all made sense of how devoted she had been to him. Their eyes locked on each other and Audrey's warm hands reached across the table and she placed her hands on top of his, tears forming in her eyes. Barry's hands turned over and grasped hers.

"Barry, from the first time I saw you at the hospital, I had a feeling that you were special. I remember you lying there looking so pale and weak. Then Father Kevin talked to me about you, and although he left me hanging when I asked more about you, he gave me the feeling, that if anyone needed to live it was you. That your life had a purpose and an unfulfilled mission."

"Did he say what that was?" Barry asked.

"No, he didn't, but I could tell it was important. I guess that's why I got so interested in you. Then, one thing led to another, and I started to have feelings for you and that's why I'm here today."

For a second, their eyes locked again. "I don't know what to say, Audrey. I like you, too, but never in my wildest dreams did I ever think…" his voice trailed off. "I guess what I'm trying to say is… you always seemed special to me, but I thought you were just being a good nurse, and I didn't want to wish for anything more than that because you were so special, and I'm just a slob down on his luck and…"

Audrey lifted her hands from his, and putting her hands on the sides of his face, pulled his head forward and kissed him softly on the lips. "I think I'm in love with this poor slob who is down on his luck," she said. "Now shut up and kiss me back."

Contrary to what Torch feared, Skip was not going to bother Doris. He had bigger fish to fry and it involved Torch. If there was one thing Skip could not tolerate, it was being threatened, and he felt right now that was what was happening. For a while he thought about skipping town and just going someplace else, but he'd had enough of that over the years. *Why,* he thought, w*as he always the one who had to be on the run?* No, he was going to stay right here in Minneapolis, and if that old detective starting getting in the way of his fun…well, he would deal with it. He had killed before and for a lot less reason.

Skip was living on the north side of Minneapolis right now, just off Lowry Avenue and Colfax, with some real low life's that looked at him as some kind of a mentor. There was a lot of money to be made in illegal drugs in Minneapolis, and he had good connections with drug traffickers down south. And now, something new—at least it was to Skip—human trafficking. Finding young girls and putting them to work taking care of the fetishes he once had, and other men were having, *Oh hell, he still had them too*, and he laughed out loud as he thought about it.

Audrey had gone home, confused, from Barry's apartment the other day. She hadn't expected him to fall head over heels in love with her on the spot, but something more than "I'll call you" would have been nice. Maybe it was all her from the start, she didn't know which, but she intended to find out. Even her daughter had asked what the problem was, and she was only ten years old. She hoped and prayed he would call.

Wednesday, the day of Barry's appointment, dawned cold and clear. It was going to be a long cold walk to the office so he had bundled up good. The doctors had told him to take care of himself. Sickness could ruin a lot of progress right now, and his immune system was badly compromised from the chemo. He thought again about Audrey as he walked to the doctor's office.

Barry had come a long way from that old ram shackled and remote log cabin in the wilderness. Living by himself in squalor up until now, and having someone tell him he was important to her—it was nice to be wanted, but it complicated things, too, because it added something into his plans he had never planned on. Audrey had taken him by surprise. *Was he ready for a relationship with a woman?* It had been so long since he had loved anyone, let alone another woman. He wasn't sure, after Kim's death, he could ever love anyone again.

Then Lisa, and still he wasn't sure how much love they had enjoyed between them. It had been more of a marriage of convenience. My God, he wasn't even sure he was going to be here a year from now. *Yes, the cancer treatments had gone well, but no one was talking about a cure. Not anyone he had talked to anyways.* When she had left the other day, Barry had said, "I'll call you." Nothing less, nothing more. He needed to think.

Barry's thoughts went in another direction. *So much unfinished business, and yes, his priorities had changed. A year ago, he would have shot Torch Brennan on sight. Maybe his newfound relationship with Father Kevin had helped heal some of his rage, and had gotten him thinking more clearly. Maybe God had touched him again and was showing him the right way to proceed. Torch Brennan didn't kill his wife. The detective had a job to do and that was to bring him to justice, even though he was innocent. Maybe his thrust should be more at finding the real killer for Torch, if he couldn't find him, and help him get his focus back where it belonged.*

He had thought a lot about his upcoming appointment with Dr. Bob. That was where he had to start. If there were secrets to be uncovered, that's where they would be. Well, tomorrow was the day he would find out and after that, he would call Audrey.

CHAPTER SIXTEEN

The office was quiet when he stepped inside and hung up his coat. Although it was very cold outside, he was sweating and wasn't sure if it was nerves from the appointment or if, maybe, he was getting sick again. He wasn't worried about it right now; he was a man on a mission. The receptionist's desk was empty but a small radio played on a little shelf next to her desk. It was some 'back to the eighties' music from a radio station in downtown Fairbanks. He picked up an old "People" magazine, opened it and thumbed through it, not stopping to look at any of the pages, and laid it back down again. He was unable, at the present moment, to concentrate or think about anything else other than his appointment. A mail carrier, bundled up for the weather, came in and tossed a pack of letters on the receptionist's desk. He nodded at Barry and smiled, but didn't say anything, and just that fast he was gone. He could hear people, in another room in the back, talking in hushed tones. He wasn't sure what it was about, but assumed it might be about him.

Barry scanned the pictures on the walls. Right now he wasn't sure if he was back in the same place he had been before. Nothing was recognizable, even though he knew he had been here before, but he had been so sick at that time that the only thing he did remember was talking with Dr. Bob, and retching with dry heaves in the bathroom. That was two months ago.

Torch and Charlie were on the walking path, strolling around Lake Calhoun. Bikers whizzed by them and joggers, some of them huffing and puffing, and others not appearing to be exerted at all, jogged by. The weather in Minnesota had been unseasonably warm for January but Torch had lived here long enough to know that could change in a hurry. When you got a warm winter day, and the sun was shining, you did your best to enjoy it. For a long time they didn't talk at all, just using their hands to convey their feelings with gentle tugs and squeezes. At last they came to a bench, by the now-deserted beach, and Charlie said, "Let's rest for a moment."

They retired to a bench next to the walking path.

"Are you unhappy that you got involved with police work again, Torch?"

"Oh, I'm not sure if 'unhappy' is the best word, dear. Frustrated... yes."

"Frustrated how, hon?"

"A lot happens when you don't wear the badge anymore. You lose a lot of your bravado, along with a lot of your power. I used to have a snitch on every corner to help me out. I didn't have to ask permission to do a lot of things, like I do now with Ray. A lot has happened since Barry was convicted, and a lot has changed. People's memories are fuzzy and they don't care anymore. They've moved on with their lives and can't see why we can't do the same."

"Do you want to quit the case?"

"Yes, but I can't because that's not the way I'm wired. Let's go get some coffee," he said, patting her knee. "Anything to change the subject."

It was Dr. Bob who came to get Barry. He sat down beside him and touched his arm. "You sure you want to do this, Barry? Sometimes these sessions will bring back things you don't want to remember. They can be painful and you've been through a lot."

"I need to do this," Barry said. "It's not a choice."

The room was dark with a medium-size video screen hung from the ceiling over a reclining chair, much like one a dentist would use. The walls were painted dark burgundy with no pictures or decorations of any kind on them. There was nothing to distract you—except what they wanted to use to prompt your mind to unload hidden secrets. The black carpet added to the gloom, as did the dark-stained woodwork. In a far corner sat a simple wooden chair, almost as if it had been an after-thought. Next to it was a laptop computer, sitting on a small wooden table.

"Please sit down and make yourself comfortable." Dr. Bob indicated the reclining chair. He fiddled with some controls until he had the chair back tilted right where he wanted it. "Are you comfortable?" he asked.

"Yes," Barry answered. If he looked up, he would be looking directly at the screen on the overhead monitor, which was dark.

Dr. Bob retreated across the room, and clearing his throat, he sat down on that solitary chair in the corner of the room, and turned on his computer. He was in front of Barry, but Barry was reclined, so the doctor was out of his line of vision.

"Barry, if this is to work it's going to take a lot of effort from both of us, so let's just go through some ground rules. I want you to concentrate on my voice and the screen above you. Don't look at me—just the screen. One of the things that has to take place for hypnosis to be successful, is for you to be completely relaxed. There will be no swinging gold watches; just some symbols on the screen that will help you take this trip backward in time. This will only be possible if you concentrate hard on what I am talking about. Do you understand?"

"Yes," Barry said.

"Okay, let's get started." He reached behind him, and shut off the overhead lights. The room went completely dark except for the light coming from his laptop screen, which reflected off the doctor's face as he concentrated on the screen.

The room was deathly quiet, save for the sound of his own breathing, and then Dr. Bob said, softly, "Barry, I need you to completely relax and let my voice help you to regress. Right now, in the center of your screen, is a red dot. That is where we are going, for within that dot lies what we are looking for. Concentrate on that dot and my voice…you are finding yourself getting very tired…you are getting tired and completely relaxed and you can feel yourself slipping willingly back in time."

Then, from the red dot, came a series of rings that formed a funnel with each ring stretching outward from the bottom, becoming bigger than the one under it. They all appeared to be spinning in a slow counter-clockwise direction. It seemed to have the same effect as a whirlpool in a river, taking you down into the depths below, but here you could see the bottom.

"Barry, you are sliding towards the big ring…I want you to enter it and then let it take you with it to the ring below…then all of the rings will ultimately take you to the red dot. Concentrate on that red dot, Barry, and let your mind go. You're very sleepy now. Trust in the rings to take you to the dot because that's where we need to be."

Unbeknownst to Barry, a small camera on the ceiling above him, was focused on his face. For Dr. Bob, it was his cue as to when Barry was totally hypnotized. Barry was fearful at first, but gradually he let go, and when he entered the big ring it was as if some angelic host had taken his hand, and was walking with him. Then, suddenly, they quit walking and just let the current take them from ring to ring. With each trip around, it seemed as if they were being propelled faster and faster. The trips were getting shorter and the rings were getting smaller. Their momentum seemed to be increasing, and he could sense they were getting closer to that elusive red dot. The dot was getting brighter, and pulsing like a living beating heart, and then, suddenly, he was inside of it and this strange calmness he had never felt before, anywhere or anytime, was taking over. It was serenity personified.

The doctor looked up and smiled. His patient was now in a trance. "Barry, I want you to think of Kim and when you first met her. You don't need to talk…just think of her…and how much you loved her and how much she loved you."

Barry's facial expression had changed from an unemotional stare to a slight smile. He had folded his hands over his chest and appeared to be relaxed.

"Now, let's think of your wedding day, and how beautiful she looked. Think of the times you talked about your future, your life together, and the family you wanted to have—the home you wanted to make together."

Barry and the doctor had discussed some things beforehand, after the last appointment, about Kim and him and their life together, so Dr. Bob knew some things about their relationship. He knew just enough to lead Barry down the subconscious path he had to take him on, to that bedroom and that night. He had to get him there subtly enough to not stir him up too much, because if that happened, Barry could awake from his trance. That could be disastrous, both to the investigation and to Barry's mental health. It was a slippery slope, indeed, and not one to be taken lightly. It was the night she died that neither Barry nor he had any idea what had happened. Neither one of them may ever know, but it was worth exploring.

He had his notes right in front of him. For the next fifteen minutes he took Barry from event to event with Kim, all of it leading up to that fateful night. Some of it seemed painful to Barry, and his facial expressions changed from time to time, smiling one minute and grimacing the next. There was perspiration showing on Barry's brow, and Dr. Bob reached up and tweaked the thermostat. He needed to keep him comfortable.

"Now, Barry, we need to talk about that last night together." He looked frightened when the doctor said this, and Bob backed off a little to let him settle down. Then resuming, he said, "You went out to celebrate your birthday that night. You had way too much to drink and Kim drove home." He had to be careful here as he was leading the witness. It needed to be Barry's words. "Do you remember coming in the house?"

"So dizzy, so drunk," Barry muttered. "Had to lie down."

"Did you go right to sleep?"

"Kim wanted to make love to me," he said. "She is naked and trying to wake me up, kissing my face and my chest. Playing with me to arouse me."

"Then what happened?"

"He's stabbing her, and slitting her throat, and the blood is gushing out. She is trying to get away, but he is holding her down by straddling her."

"Can't you help her?"

"Nothing works anymore."

"Do you see his face?"

"I do, but I don't know him."

"Then what happened?" Tears were streaming down Barry's face.

"He fondled her and then he dressed her in her pajamas."

"Did he leave?"

"No, he came to my side of the bed and held the knife over my neck. He stood there for a long time, breathing hard and looking at me."

"Then what happened?"

"Then he went back to her side of the bed, and wiped the knife off on her pajama top, and put the knife in my hand..."

"You still don't know him?"

Barry didn't answer, and he seemed extremely sad, almost anguished. His hands were balled into fists and he held them by his sides.

"Barry, answer me—who is he?"

"From Flagg's. He has a uniform on, and the patch on the sleeve says 'Flagg's.'" With that, Barry curled into a fetal position and sobbed.

It was time to wake him up. Dr. Bob shut off the equipment and went over to stand next to him. "Barry, I will count to ten. When you hear the word 'ten' the next time, you will wake up." Dr. Bob then proceeded to count to ten, and Barry woke up, frightened and disoriented.

"Let's give you a few minutes, and then we'll go over the tape." He squeezed Barry's shoulder and left the room. In a few minutes, he was back and said, "Let's go in my office." It was right across the hall. "Coffee?" he said, as Barry made himself comfortable on a leather couch.

"Sounds good. Just black, please."

CHAPTER SEVENTEEN

Barry had gone home after the appointment and fallen asleep for some time. It was now dark outside, and in the room, as he sat on the edge of the bed trying to think about what he wanted to do next. *Call Audrey,* he thought. He rubbed his eyes and reached for the phone. The phone rang four times, and then her answering machine picked up. "Hi, I'm not home right now but please leave your number and a message. Thanks."

He waited for the signal—not sure what he wanted to say or what he was going to say, but before he could formulate anything, the machine was prompting him. "Audrey, hi, I'm home right now. Feeling kind of drained, but I could use someone to talk to if you're not busy." He hung the phone up and sat back down. Dr. Bob had taken time to go over the tapes with him in his office. Barry was disappointed that he hadn't been able to recognize anyone, but was relieved that it was someone else, and not he, that killed Kim—although he had never believed he did. A copy of the tape lay on the end of his bed.

They had discussed the statement that Barry had made while under hypnosis, that the killer was wearing some kind of patch with a flag. Was the man a cop or some public servant who wore the flag on the shoulder of his uniform? "Who would kill while in uniform?" The doctor had said.

Barry hadn't tried to correct him. The man he saw in his subconscious mind wasn't wearing a patch with a flag, his uniform patch said, 'Flagg's.' He was keeping that to himself. The name on that patch clearly rang a bell with him.

He busied himself cleaning up the apartment. Maybe he would call work and see if they had anything for him to do. Construction slowed down a lot in the winter but Curt had told him as soon as he felt well enough, to give him a call. Just then the phone rang.

"Hi," she said. "Sorry I missed your call but I went to pick my daughter up from school. How did it go at the doctor's office?"

"Okay," Barry said. "Can I come over? I need to talk."

"Sure," Audrey said. "Anytime would be fine. I have hamburger out and we can have some burgers."

"Sound good," Barry said. "See you in few minutes."

Doctor Bob and Father Kevin sat in the doctor's office, drinking single malt scotch and smoking cigars. It was a way for both of them to unwind after a hard day at the office. He had called the priest shortly after Barry had left, and asked him to come over. They had been friends for a long time, and they both had an interest in Barry's case.

"I can tell you, with all certainty, Father, that Barry Winston did not kill his wife. The subconscious mind under hypnosis will not lie. So where we go from here, I don't know. To hear Barry tell it, he has been convicted of killing his wife in a court of law. For us to harbor him is a crime, even though he is an innocent man. Barry knows I can't protect him any longer. I guess I am asking for your advice. I could lose my license if I am found harboring a fugitive."

Father Kevin set his empty glass down and wiped his lips on the sleeve of his coat. "When I first met Barry, and he told me his story, I gave some thought to getting in touch with some friends I have back in Minneapolis. I came from that area, you know."

"I didn't," the doctor said, pouring himself another drink and offering the bottle to his friend.

Father Kevin held his hand up, indicating he had enough. "I think I am going to get in touch with them now, and see if they can tell me if there has been any change in the arrest warrant. I know that may be tipping our hand to the police, but perhaps we can get Barry out of here, to some safer location, until we can find out what we need to do. Maybe if they knew what we know, they might give Barry a new trial. Either way, I have to get going, but I'll let you know what I find out. In the meantime, I guess, unless the police contact you, you don't have to say anything to anybody. It's not lying to just be quiet."

"I'll remember that the next time I go to confession," he said.

Father Kevin laughed long and hard. He had to get back to the church. They would be coming for food and shelter soon. It was another cold night in Fairbanks.

Barry walked up the steps and rang the bell. He was pushing snow off to the side with his foot as heard her coming to the door. Audrey reached up and kissed him on the end of the nose as she opened the door. "Hurry," she said, "You'll let the heat out."

Her daughter smiled at him, but quickly went back to watching some kids' program on television.

"Come in the kitchen," she said, "where we can talk." She poured him coffee and put some cookies out. "How long was your session?" she asked.

"Oh, I'm not sure, but most of the afternoon."

"And?" She was sitting across from him with a quizzical look on her face.

Barry fidgeted in his chair. Finally, he said, "Audrey, I think I need to move on." I know that the only person who is going to find the man that killed Kim is me. I also know that, by now, they may or may not know where I am. If I get caught then all is lost."

"Where would you go?" she asked.

"Back to Minneapolis," he said, "to find Kim's killer."

"Barry, can I change the subject?" she asked. She had a hurt look on her face and she went to the door and looked in the other room at her daughter. "Do you have feelings for me?" she asked, with tears welling in her eyes. She didn't sit back down across from him, but stood beside him, looking down at him, but not touching him.

Barry had felt that this line of questioning would be coming. He didn't have an answer. *Yes, he did have feelings for her, but he was caught between a rock and a hard place. Maybe it was a couple of rocks and a hard place. One of the rocks was finding Kim's killer and the other rock was his own illness that he felt was just in remission, waiting to come back and silence him for good.* "Audrey, I do care for you. It's just…"

"Just what, Barry?"

He got up and tried to hold her. She was crying openly now, but she would have no part of it and pushed him away.

"Audrey, will you give me six months. I don't want to lose you, but you have to understand, I can't live the rest of my life running from the law. I need to clear this up," and now he was starting to tear up, too. She sat down and he was standing over her. "Honey," he said now, holding her hands. "Please trust me to come back, and if the cancer doesn't get me, I want nothing more than to live the rest of my life with you and your daughter. I want to be the father she has never had, and the husband you always wanted. I want us both to live in happiness for the rest of our lives, but I have to find Kim's killer and take care of this injustice. I can't go on any longer with him being free, and myself being hunted."

Audrey had dried her dark eyes and now had a tissue balled up in her hand. "What are you going to do when you find him, Barry?"

"I don't know right now. That will depend on the police and him."

"Will you kill him?"

"If that's the only way, yes."

"What about your treatments, Barry?"

"I talked to the hospital and they are going to send my records down to Minneapolis as soon as I pick out a hospital. The oncologist felt I would be fine for the next few weeks."

Audrey had talked to his doctors, too, and she knew all about this.

She stood up, and they passionately kissed and embraced each other. Finally, he pulled himself away, tenderly holding her head with his hands, and staring at her. "I will be back, sweetheart," he whispered.

"When are you going?"

"Tomorrow, right after I see Father Kevin." Then he dropped his hands and put his coat back on. "Pray for me," he said.

"Barry, stay the night, please. I want to hold you for just one night before you go."

"No. I want to Audrey. God knows how much I want to, but I can't. You have to believe me and trust me." He kissed her again and then, holding her at arm's length, they just stared at each other through tear-rimmed eyes.

She watched him walk away from the building, his breath showing in the frigid Alaskan air. He wasn't walking towards home; he was going to the church. "Please God," she prayed, "bring him back to me."

Father Kevin sat with Barry in his office. Up to this time, he wasn't sure what Barry's intentions had been. He had wanted to help him a long time ago, after Barry had told him the story of Kim. Then the cancer came along, and for a while, it seemed to be a moot point. But right now, he wanted to help him if he could.

"I mentioned a while back that I came from Minneapolis before I was sent to Alaska. I might be able to arrange for a place for you to stay for a while if that would help you."

"Thanks, Father, but right now I think the fewer people I involve, the better. However, if it is some place where I can remain inconspicuous, it would sure help. I need to stay as private as I can. My biggest problem right now is I'm broke, so I need to borrow some money to get there. I was going to ask Aud..." he broke off in the middle of the word. "I was going to ask this girl I know, but I don't think she has much more than I do."

"I know about Audrey, Barry. I'll loan you the money."

"Just a few hundred and air fare would do it. I'll find some work when I get there and get you paid back. I don't imagine priests have a lot of money. I do want to come back here after this is all cleared up."

"Let's pray together before you leave."

They went into the church, and both knelt down in the back pew. The church was dark, except for some votive candles burning in two racks at the back. Father Kevin took Barry's hand in his as he prayed," God, we ask for a safe journey for this man. We ask that he find justice, without having to hurt anybody except maybe the guilty. We ask that his body will stay cleansed of the cancer that has befallen him. We ask that you would bring him back to us, safe and sound." They both sat back and then he put his arm around Barry, "God be with you, my friend." He squeezed his shoulder, and then got up and left Barry sitting there. For a while, Barry's mind was reeling. So much had happened in the last two days. He needed to go pack and call the airport. Father Kevin appeared once more, and gave him an envelope with a thousand dollars in it, in twenty-dollar bills. "Godspeed, my friend. There is an address in there of a friend of mine, and his phone number. He will do what he can to help you. I've already called him about your need to remain inconspicuous."

"Thank you, Father. I will pay you back as soon as I get back here."
They hugged briefly and Barry left, heading back to his apartment for
his last night there. That is, if he could get a flight out the next day.

Torch hadn't worked on the case for a few days. Not that he had
anything to do, or any leads to follow, anyway. He was at a standstill.
It was a cold case that seemed to be getting colder every day. The
thought of shelving the whole thing, and just getting back on with
his retirement, had crossed his mind more than once. He was stupid
to get involved in this crap again. All those years he had waited for
retirement, and then didn't know how to handle it. In fact, maybe he
should go see Ray and tell him to shove it. Maybe he had learned a
few lessons about what not to do in retirement. No matter how bored
you get, don't go back to where you came from. Find something new
and exciting. He hadn't tried hard enough to find that something, and
Charlie had brought that up the other day. He pulled over to the side
of the street as he was driving home from lunch with a friend, and
dialed Ray's number.

"Homicide," Ray answered.

"Ray, Torch—you busy?"

"Always busy, my friend, but what do you want?"

"I want to talk to you about the Barry Winston case."

"Well, I want to talk to you about Barry Winston, too, because we
just got a tip from a contractor in Alaska who says he was working
for him."

"Where in Alaska, and how come you're sitting on this?"

"Just crossed my desk, Torch. I was going to call you as soon I
had time. As for where—Fairbanks."

"Fairbanks. Ain't that damn cold up there this time of the year?"

"Freeze the balls off a brass monkey, Torch, but all you got to do
is go get him and bring him back. I'm not sending you on a damn
vacation. Now, what the hell else did you want to tell me about,
Barry?"

"Nothing."

"Well, come on in. I'll fill you in and you can fly out tomorrow."

"Okay, I'll be there in fifteen minutes."

Skip had left town but he would be back. He was just going down to South Carolina to settle a score with a snitch. *Teach him to screw with old Skip.*

Before he came to Minneapolis, Skip had opened his mouth and talked too much while he was down there. He had done a little bragging that he shouldn't have done. Now this guy was blackmailing him and saying he was going to the cops unless Skip came up with some cash and fast. Skip called the guy and said he was coming down. He would make things right with him, but for now, he was to keep his lips sealed. The guy's name was Darien Frisco. Darien didn't know it, but he had one day to live.

Skip's entire life had been a mess. When he was four, he had been beaten so badly by his father that he lost some of his hearing. He was taken out of school at age seven because he wasn't able to hear the teacher. His parents, or at that time his mother because his dad had been killed in a drive-by shooting, either wouldn't or couldn't get him some help with his hearing problem. Left home alone to entertain himself because his mother was out whoring herself for drugs, he spent hours killing birds and small animals with an air pellet gun. When he was thirteen, he molested the neighbor girl, who was eight. When he was fifteen, his mother started having sex with him because she felt, if she did, he would leave the other girls alone. He watched pornography in his spare time, which just enhanced his misguided desires.

When he was sixteen, he raped his first girl, but it went unreported. That was the first of a long string of sex crimes—each of them getting more violent because he couldn't stand the thought that any girl would refuse his advances, and those who balked, would be punished. All too soon, it wasn't just the girl submitting to him, but he tried prostituting them with other men, for money.

The gal he had killed in Charleston was another one who felt his wrath, and found out you don't just dump Skip Hendricks, or tell him you won't work for him. He had sex with her, and then he strangled her and threw her body in the Ashley River, right in the middle of town. The cops had arrested him because he was the last person seen with her, but they couldn't prove anything. Same old story, just some circumstantial evidence. They made him submit a DNA sample, but they couldn't find any of his on, or in her. A week in the river had ruined that. He hadn't killed since, but he wasn't afraid to kill again if he had to. His mistake had come when he told Darien, one night at a drunken party, what a big splash she made when she hit the river. Then a phone call came from Darien to Skip for a loan, and when Skip told him to go to hell, the subsequent threat to tell the Charleston police about the girl.

The seatbelt lights came on and the pilot said, "We are starting our decent. It's fifty-six degrees and raining lightly in Charleston. Thank you for flying with us."

Skip gathered up his stuff and watched out the window for the runway lights. He needed to get some sleep, so a good hotel would be his first stop.

For some reason, in the cab on the way to the hotel, he thought of Kim again. *It had been so many years. He seldom thought about her, but it was the cops that kept bringing her up, not him. He had killed Kim because she thought she was too damn good for him, just like the others. For a while, he felt he had screwed up because he hadn't killed Barry, too, when he had the chance; but the blundering cops had made it all right, hadn't they, and Barry got charged instead of him.*

Now it was Darien's turn. He didn't like killing men but he didn't like going to jail, either, and now he needed to take care of business. His face was pressed against the cool glass of the airplane window as he saw the lights of Charleston International airport below them. He was going through a mental checklist as the plane descended.

His first stop after the hotel and a good night's sleep would be to call a cab and find a different hotel. Then he would call Darien and arrange for a meeting.

CHAPTER EIGHTEEN

Torch was flying out to Fairbanks in the morning. Last night, he and Charlie had talked long into the night about the chance to arrest Barry and bring this whole thing to a close. He wasn't elated or even excited about the prospect of catching him. He just wanted to get it over with; to bring him back where he belonged, to the state penitentiary in Oak Park Heights, or to prove him innocent.

Fairbanks police would make the arrest so there was no danger to Torch, but he would be bringing him back alone. They were going to wait until tomorrow to bust him, when Torch got there, because he had asked them to do that. He just wanted to see the look on Barry's face when they knocked on that door. He had all the details worked out in his head. This wasn't the first time he had brought a fugitive home, but it was going to be the last. For Torch, it was going to be the last piece of the puzzle.

He pounded his pillow into a ball; sleep was going to come hard tonight. He reached over and touched Charlie's arm but she was fast asleep and shivered slightly when he touched her. Then the sleeping pill kicked in and he drifted off.

Barry was on his way to Fairbanks International in a cab. His ticket to Minneapolis was a one-way ticket, but he had no intention of staying there after he found the man who killed his wife. He was coming back to Fairbanks and Audrey, if he lived that long. Yesterday he had his final visit with the oncologist at the hospital and told him he was going to be gone for while. He was careful to not say where at first, but when pressed because he was told he would need ongoing testing and oversight, he said, "Minneapolis."

"That's good," the doctor said. "I have a friend who is an oncologist at University Hospital on the campus there. I will brief him on your case, and give you his information." He was writing it down as he talked.

Barry looked at the slip of paper. Dr. John Timken was his name, and he was at the University Cancer Hospital. "Thank you," he said. "I hope to be back before the cancer is back."

"You're in remission now, my friend. Let's hope it stays that way for a long time." After Barry had left, the doctor looked at the file and Barry's test results again. The results certainly didn't spell out a cure, as there were still cancer cells evident, but he should be fine for a while.

Audrey sat in her cubicle at her nursing station. She was confused, but adamant, that she was doing the right thing. The hospital was not going to tell her whom she could and couldn't see.

The conclusion she had come to, as to the 'why' she was in love with this man; he was sick and would probably die at some point in the not too distant future. *Was it just pity for Barry? No, she didn't think so.* She had loved before and she knew what it felt like. The man she had loved back then had not been the kind and considerate sort of man Barry was. In fact, he was the opposite. She felt at the time she could change him, but that had not worked out and he had abused her terribly. *Now, sometimes*, she thought, *she despised him*. But he had given her Sarah, had he not? That beautiful little daughter she lived for every day. Right now, she needed someone to love, and so did Sarah.

Bells in the hallway, and a call over the speakers for Code Blue in Room 314, brought her out of her daydream. She grabbed the crash cart and headed down the hall. Other nurses were coming from the opposite direction.

Torch had never been in Fairbanks before, and although Minnesota wasn't known for a warm climate, it was like a sauna compared to the icy blast that hit him in the face as he left the terminal at Fairbanks International. A shrill whistle got his attention, and there was an unmarked with a young officer holding his picture in his hand. "You Torch?" he asked. "I got orders to give you a ride down to headquarters."

Skip had a change of plans come his way when he talked to Darien. Darien didn't want to meet him anywhere but at the hotel Skip was staying at. He was adamant about it. He was coming to the hotel this evening to meet him, and would wait for him in the lobby. He needed money and he needed it fast. His only stipulation to the meeting was that the whole thing had to take place in a public setting. He didn't want to be alone with Skip. The man's reputation preceded him and he just plain didn't trust him.

The cab dropped Skip off at the entrance to the Travelers Inn, but not before he stopped at a hardware store and purchased a cylinder of propane, telling the driver to wait and he would be right back.

The hotel had been around for many years, and it was showing its age, but the old "Vacancy" sign still glowed softly in the waning light of the late afternoon. The white stucco building looked yellow from age, and from the water from the outside sprinkler system. The red tile roof appeared almost orange. He fished a twenty out of his pocket and gave it to the driver, who looked at the $19.10 reading on the meter, and looked back at his passenger for more, but he was already leaving the cab. Disgusted, he threw the car into gear and squealed out of the cobblestone driveway muttering, "Cheap ass."

He paged through some of the ID cards, in his billfold, until he found the right one, the one he had especially made for this trip. He went inside to the registration desk and said, "I would like a room for the night," pushing the South Carolina driver's license across the counter.

"Just one night?" the tired-looking clerk asked. "That will be sixty one dollars, Mr. Frisco," he said, scanning the card before he gave it back to him."

Skip didn't answer him but handed him three twenties and a five.

The clerk pushed a white card across the counter. "Fill out the front and sign the back. You'll be in three fourteen. Checkout time tomorrow is noon."

Skip filled out the card and gave it back to him, and he gave Skip a room card for the door lock. "Have a nice night," he said, glancing at the card and putting it into a bin—not noticing that Frisco was spelled Fresco.

Skip was laying on the bed, thinking. He had no money to give Darien. Somehow, he needed to make him think he did. Somehow, he had to get him away from the hotel lobby, and he didn't want to be seen there with him. He knew Darien was a cocaine junkie and that might be his key. Darien needed a fix bad...he had heard it in his voice. Skip had four ounces of the purest coke on the market, and he had been saving it for just such a time. Skip occasionally used cocaine himself, but was far from being addicted. He had his own special addiction, and it didn't involve drugs, it involved young girls and violence.

Torch had never been so damn cold in all of his life. He turned to the young cop and said, "You guys got to be out of your frosty minds to live up here. How damn cold is it?"

"Forty three below," the cop laughed. "You'll get used to it."

"Bull shit," Torch said, "I'm going to arrest this guy and get the hell back on a plane yet today. I'm from Minnesota and we get cold, too, but not for eight months at a time. You should just leave this crap to the Eskimos and polar bears."

The cop just laughed. The first stop was the police station, where a detective and two uniformed officers were waiting. Then it was just a short drive over to Barry's apartment. They headed uptown, the car's tires squeaking in the freshly fallen snow.

The detective, Larry Neilson, had been in Fairbanks for seven years now. He'd worked in Canada before, for the Royal Canadian Mounted Police and still held dual citizenship. He introduced himself to Torch saying, "We could have just arrested this bird for you and sent him back, unless you came up for the scenery."

Torch smiled. "You can have the scenery, my friend. I just want to get my man. It's kind of a personal thing with me. This guy and I go back a long way."

"I understand. We checked on him two days ago. I'm sure he has no inkling you're coming for him."

"I hope not," Torch said. "You will have to make the arrest for me. I'm not officially a cop anymore."

"Bounty hunter?" the detective asked.

"You might say that," Torch answered. He didn't want to explain any further.

They parked right in front of the building. The two uniformed cops went first, although they weren't expecting any trouble. The door to his apartment was open, and a young woman was packing a few things in boxes. Torch approached her and identified himself, putting his hand on her arm. "Is this Barry Winston's apartment?" Torch asked, his eyes taking in the rest of the rooms as he talked.

"Yes," she answered, looking visibly flustered.

"Where is he and who are you?" Torch asked. One of the uniformed cops took her arm.

"My name is Audrey Snyder, and I have no idea where he is and let go of me."

"Then what are you doing here?" Torch was getting upset and it showed in his face.

"He asked me to store a few things for him."

"But you don't know where he is?" Torch was almost chest-to-chest with her now.

"No...No, I don't, and that's all I have to say." Audrey looked as if she was going to cry.

The other uniform came back in the room. "No sign of him anywhere, guys," he said. "But I did find this." He was holding up a sheet of paper on which was written 'Flight 657 to Minneapolis. Leaves 9:35.'

Torch looked at his watch—it was 8:15.

"Call the airport and have security hold that flight," Torch said. "No one leaves the boarding area until we get there. You come with us," he said to Audrey. "We want to talk to you. You probably better not say anything until we read you your rights."

Audrey was crying openly now, but she did as Torch asked, and didn't say anything.

The Fairbanks detective put his phone back in his pocket. "That flight left yesterday, Torch."

Torch reached in his jacket pocket and took out his flight information and let out a big sigh. He had come up on flight 657, which was the same plane Barry had gotten off of in Minneapolis, when Torch had boarded the plane.

CHAPTER NINTEEN

Skip was waiting in the parking lot when Darien showed up. He had been careful to stay out of the view of the security cameras. He didn't want to be seen together with him. A soft rain was falling, and you could see it sparkle in the parking lot lights. Darien was alone so that was good. Skip shivered and pulled his shirt collar up. He wasn't sure if he was cold or just scared. He had to approach his foe before he went inside, and he was getting out of his car right now.

"Darien." He jerked his head around at the voice coming from the shadows by the building. Two young women, obviously intoxicated, came out of the entrance to the left, kissed passionately and left in opposite directions. For a second, they interrupted Skip's train of thought. *He hated gay women worse than the others, but not now,* he thought.

"Darien, I want to make things right with you," he said, putting his hands on the younger man's shoulders. "I don't like being blackmailed, but I do owe you some thanks, so listen to what I want to do. You want to go up to my room where we can talk?"

"We can talk here," Darien said. His eyes were bloodshot and his hands were trembling.

"You need a fix, buddy?" Skip asked.

"Not from you," Darien said. Skip looked around—they were all alone. He took a small mirror out of his pocket and poured out a small amount of coke onto the face of it. "Here, let's take the edge off," he said, rolling up a ten-dollar bill to use for a snort tube, and handing it to Darien. "Hurry up before it gets all wet," he said.

Darien rubbed his eyes. He didn't want to do this but one line wouldn't hurt.

"This is high grade stuff," Skip said. "Lots more where that came from."

He put one hand on Skip's shoulder to balance himself, as the rush came over him. *This was some good shit,* he thought. Skip was holding onto his arm and they were walking away from the entrance towards an exit door, on the side of the building, that appeared to be open just a crack. It was the same door Skip had come out of after disabling the built-in alarm by cutting a wire to a battery. At the bottom of the door was a small dead tree branch that prevented it from closing.

Barry was back in the city he once loved—the homeland. He was staying at the rectory of Father Kevin's friend, Father Paul Larson. He had a hopeless task at hand, but he had to try. Try and find the man, with a Flagg's patch on his uniform, who killed his wife.

Audrey waved her right to an attorney. She had done nothing wrong and had nothing to hide. They knew Barry had left for Minnesota and so did she. They didn't know where in Minnesota he went, and neither did she. Barry had not told her anything, only that he was leaving and he would be back for her.

"Are you romantically joined?" Torch asked. "No, let me rephrase that poor choice of words, are you friends?"

"Yes," she said.

"Is it serious?"

"It is to me."

"How about to him?" Torch couldn't figure out if she was just being elusive or not, but thought he might be able to break the ice with her if he could gain her confidence.

"I'm not sure how he feels about me," Audrey said. "I think he likes me."

"Do you know why we're after him?"

"Yes, he told me."

"He told you he was wanted, but did he tell you why?"

Audrey hesitated. She had to be careful here as she could implicate others.

Torch would skip that question for now. "Where do you work, Audrey?"

"At the hospital. I'm a nurse."

"Is that where you met Barry?"

"Yes, that's where we met."

"Was he a patient?"

"Yes."

"What was wrong with him, or should I assume he was sick or hurt?"

"I can't tell you that. It's confidential and I could lose my job."

"Yes, sorry. We'll check with the hospital." It was Torch's way of saying, "I'll find out one way or another."

Audrey started crying again, and Torch slid a box of Kleenex her way. She was pretty in a petite sort of way. He was starting to feel sorry he was putting her though this.

"He didn't do what you think he did," she blurted out.

"He didn't do what?"

"Kill his wife. He's gone back to find the real killer. The job you should be doing and not him," she wailed, and hit the table with her hand. She was crying hard and put her head down.

"What makes you think he's innocent, besides him saying he is?"

"Because I know him well and he couldn't do that, but…Oh, what the hell!" she exclaimed, raising her head back up. "Talk to Dr. Bob. He'll explain it."

"Does Dr. Bob have a last name, and where is his office?"

"Dr. Bob Holden, and his office is down on Front Street. Can I leave? I have to pick up my daughter from school."

Torch reached across and took her hand. "I'm sorry about this. Yes, go get your daughter, and if you think of anything else that could help us, please call me." He wrote the number of the Fairbanks police office on the back, copying it from another card he had, and handed it to her. "I hope he didn't do it, but I need to prove that, and I need to find him to help me prove that. You have to understand that, Audrey."

She rose and slipped out the door without answering him. The same cop who picked Torch up at the airport was waiting to take her back to her car.

Darien was out on his feet but Skip got under his arm and helped him into the elevator. He had given him just one line of cocaine, but it was uncut and pretty strong, and he was really out of it. Once inside the room, Skip dumped him on the bed and went to work, preparing him another treat.

In his pocket, he had a small bottle of solvent, which he would use to purify the cocaine. Then he would inject Darien with a dose that would rock his world one last time. The heater was the small propane torch he'd purchased on the way. He mixed the coke and solvent and brought it to a boil in a spoon he had in his pocket. Darien was sleeping it off, and not aware of what was going on, as Skip fastened a rubber strap around his arm. An arm already filled with old puncture wounds from previous injections.

Skip drew up a syringe full of the liquid, waited a second for it to cool, tapped it to settle the bubbles, and then injected it into Darien's limp arm.

He reacted almost immediately, sitting up in bed and glaring at Skip, his mouth wide open but no sound coming out. Then he fell to his right side, his upper half landing on the floor, and his legs still on the bed. He let out a groan and immediately went into a seizure as the overdose found its way to his brain. He convulsed several times and then quit breathing.

Skip wiped everything down, that he had touched, with a wad of wet toilet paper he had gotten from the bathroom; the burner, the tank and the syringe, and left the needle in Darien's arm. Then he flushed the paper and the rest of the cocaine down the toilet, but not before he did a small line for himself. He sat in a chair looking out the window, thinking about what had just happened, while he enjoyed the drug. This part of town was closing up for the night. Traffic past the hotel was virtually nonexistent on the wet shiny streets. There was another hotel a few blocks away. He would check in there and get a cab to the airport in the morning.

Rising from the chair, he went and stood over Darien's body. "That's what you get for blackmailing Skip," he muttered. He looked around the room once more, mentally going over everything. He patted his shirt pocket...the room card...where was it? He saw it on the nightstand where he had left it. *That's as good a place as any,* he thought. He went over to the door, his flight bag in his hand, and turned off the light, closing the door softly behind him.

When Barry got off the flight in Minneapolis, he quickly walked out of the airport and hailed a cab. Pulling a slip of paper from his pocket, he found the address Father Kevin had given him. "427 Larch," he said to the driver.

"Is that up by the Basilica?" the driver asked.

"I think so," he answered. "I've never been there."

The area around the airport had changed over the years, but there were still landmarks that were familiar to him. On his left was old Fort Snelling, as they made their way north on Hiawatha Ave. and to his right, the Mississippi River Valley where the Mississippi wound its way downstream to St. Paul.

His plan was to find a place to stay, and Father Kevin had told him his friend would help him with that. Then he would do some detective work. He needed to visit a courier service called Flagg's, and see what they could share with him.

Skip was suffering from remorse, which was a new feeling for him. His thoughts had been on Darien, as he walked the three blocks to the Inn he had checked into, earlier. Darien had been an old friend for many years. They had done so many things together, and at one point, were almost like brothers. But there was no room in Skip's life for friendship when that friend was trying to blackmail him, was there? Then the reasoning kicked in again, and he knew that was not really Darien talking, but the drug talking. It was the addiction, the cravings that drove you to do things you never would think about when your mind was right. *Would Darien actually have turned him in to the police? He didn't think so, but he couldn't take the chance.* He walked up the drive to the Old Stone Inn. He needed some sleep.

The meeting had been put together very hastily the next day, in a conference room at the Fairbanks Police Station. In the room were Dr. Bob Holden, Father Kevin, Audrey and Torch. The meeting was Torch's idea, but it was Audrey that had pulled all of the players together. This was after she had told Torch of Barry's medical condition.

Torch was talking with Audrey. "How did you meet Barry?"

She put her coffee cup down. "I met him at the hospital when he came in for cancer treatment."

"Where had he been living before that?"

"At the church," Father Kevin interrupted. "He stayed at the church for a while until he got a job in construction, and then he rented a small apartment up on Front Street."

"Where before that?" Torch asked.

"Out in the sticks, I guess. He never fully explained where he came from. He just told me that he was a fugitive."

"Was he very sick when you met him?" He was back to talking with Audrey.

"I would say so. He was dying, in my estimation, but I'm not a doctor. Liver cancer is always serious."

He shifted his focus back to Father Kevin. "Was he sick when he met you?"

The young priest shifted in his chair. "I would say so, detective. Like I said, we run a homeless shelter at the church, and he was looking for someplace to stay. He didn't look well at that time, but I'm pretty sure he hadn't yet sought help for his illness."

"Did he confide his past to you?"

"Yes, he shared a lot of it, but some of that I can't talk about without his permission. It was in the form of a confession."

"Did he say what he…" Torch waved his hand. "Forget it, I don't want to know."

Torch turned to the doctor. "Dr. Bob—you had a chance to treat him and question him. What was your role and why did he come to you?"

"I had the opportunity to use hypnosis to help him find out what had happened in his past."

"He was searching for answers?" Torch asked.

"Yes, he was. He wasn't awake that night when his wife was killed, but he was there, inebriated and helpless. He saw more than he thought he saw."

Torch looked at Father Kevin and Audrey. "Can I talk to the doctor alone?" he asked. They both got up and left the room.

"Please stay for a few more minutes," Torch told them as they stepped outside the door. "This won't take long."

Back in the room, he turned to the doctor. "What can you share with me about your findings, doctor? Keep in mind, if it's something that exonerates Barry, it's important."

"I can tell you that he didn't kill his wife, but that's about all I can tell you."

"Is that a hunch, a guess or medical science?" Torch asked.

"That's my professional opinion. Yes, I would say it's science, detective."

Torch called the other two back in. "Can anyone tell me where he went?"

"Minneapolis," Audrey said.

"Can you be more specific?"

"Audrey shook her head."

Torch turned to Father Kevin, but didn't ask him the same question. "Father, what if I told you I would like to find him, to prove his innocence?"

Father shook his head. "I hope you do, detective, I hope you do. But right now, I think the only one that can prove him innocent is Barry, and I'd like to see him get the chance to do that. Your catching him is not going to accomplish that. Why don't you work with him instead of against him?"

Torch didn't answer the priest, but he thought to himself, *he has a point.*

Torch addressed the whole group. "I've learned a lot of things today I didn't know. I want you all to know how much I appreciate your input. Please call me if you have anything else you can add to this."

Skip was restless that night and sleep was not coming. He finally took another line of coke to calm himself down. *Why couldn't Darien have kept his mouth shut,* he thought. *I really didn't want to have to kill him.*

Housekeeping, at the motel, found Darien's body the next morning about 11:30. The petite middle-aged Asian woman went screaming down the hallway until her supervisor found her and calmed her down. Then they called the Charleston Police, and Detective Clarence Kemper was assigned to the case. He estimated the man had been dead about twelve hours and it looked like an overdose of cocaine, but they would have an autopsy preformed. That was routine. You could never take things at their face value. Nothing in the room, however, suggested anything else.

The front desk confirmed that Darien Fresco had checked in last night and they gave the detective the registration card he had signed. He gave it a cursory glance and put it in his pocket. "Were you the one who checked him in?" he asked the clerk.

"No, that would have been Simpson. He doesn't come in until three and tonight is his night off. Do you want his phone number?"

"Yeah. No, wait, I'll come back and see him if I need anything else. The lab boys will be in the room for about an hour and then it's yours." He turned and walked out the door to his waiting car.

Two days later, the autopsy report and the lab work were back, with some unanswered questions. Detective Kemper sat at his desk going over the results.

It was death by overdose, but from the residue they found on the needle, which was still in his arm, it was a very pure dose of cocaine. For all practical purposes, it was uncut. Not something you saw too often in users in this area. The other inconsistency was fingerprints. Someone had wiped the propane bottle clean. Darien would not have been able to hold it while cooking the coke, without getting his prints on it, and going back even farther on a metal surface like this, there should have been other prints—like the people who worked in the store, or the manufacturer. Also, no container for the cocaine or the solvent was found.

There was one other thing that was troubling. Darien's prints were not on the room card. There were two sets of prints on it, but not Darien's, and they were working right now to find out whose prints they were. They did not use the cards over, so one set could be presumed to be the clerk who issued the card.

Kemper took out the registration slip from the file that the desk had given him. That's when he noticed the name was spelled wrong. *This guy might have been a doper, but he should have been able to spell his own name.* He looked at the signature on Darien Frisco's driver's license that had been in his wallet. They didn't match.

Stopping at the receptionist's desk, Kemper said, "I will be out at the Traveler's Inn by the airport if anyone needs me."

CHAPTER TWENTY

Father Ryan Murphy, who had an Irish brogue that made you listen closely, had picked up Barry at the airport. He was middle-aged with a lot of gray creeping into his red hair, and bushy eyebrows that went up and down with his ever-changing facial expressions. He talked very fast and in short blurbs, and accented his speech with his hands, which often left the steering wheel as he weaved in and out of the traffic, not paying much attention to other drivers. He was acting as if he was riding in the car, not driving it, but he greeted Barry as if he was an old long lost friend.

In the car, on the way back to the rectory, he explained that he and Father Kevin had become very close while in the seminary together and talked quite often. He had never been assigned to a parish, preferring to stay at the school teaching theology. "I'm so happy to be able to help a friend of Kevin's. You can stay until your business is completed," he said. He didn't mention if he knew what that business was or if he even cared.

The rectory, where Father Murphy resided, was in between the church and one of the other school buildings, but a separate building onto itself. The other buildings, that were dormitories, were more like apartment buildings sitting around the outer edge of the huge stone house of worship, but all of them were joined by covered walkways that made getting around easier in the cold Minnesota winters. Two other educational buildings were on the grounds, but separated by some distance, making the area look more like they were part of a small campus that had been added later. Inside the rectory was a large lobby area filled with furniture, and several priests in their traditional black, and monks in brown robes, were engaged in conversation. Down the hall, in what he could only assume was a chapel in the church itself, he could hear men's voices singing in some kind of a religious litany.

"I'll show you to your quarters and give you some time to clean up, Barry. Supper will be at seven in the commissary, but I'll meet you right here a little before and then show you around the grounds and buildings."

"Thank you," he said. "You don't know how much I appreciate this. Is there a computer I can use to look up some information?"

"There is one in the room," Father Murphy replied. "I'll show you how to get on it."

Barry had a list of the places he wanted to go as soon as he could make arrangements. The first place would be to pick up a rental car, and then he wanted to visit the offices of Flagg's courier service. He wasn't sure if anyone would give out information to a common citizen, but that wasn't going to stop him from trying. The other person he wanted to talk with was a friend of Kim's from the beauty shop. He had wanted to talk to her before the trial, but never got a chance to because she was so angry with him having, supposedly, killed Kim, that she refused to talk to him. Hopefully, that had changed. Her name was Cheryl Cousins. His biggest fear was she would call the cops on him. He was going to have to be careful, but something told him she had part of the key that would unlock the mystery.

Using the computer at the rectory, Barry was able to find out that Flagg's was now called Twin City Parcel Service. A quick phone call told him they were not going to be much help because their files were confidential, but if he wanted to stop by they would be glad to help him as much as they could, within the law. He made an appointment for the next day at 10:00 a.m.

That night, Barry had supper with several of the priests and monks, who talked to him at great length about the Alaskan wilderness where he had lived. Most of them had never been out of the metropolitan area having, at a young age, dedicated their lives to prayer and meditation to God.

At last he excused himself and went to bed, exhausted, and almost immediately fell into a deep sleep. Once again, his mind went back to that horrible night. At first, his dream was all foggy as it had been in the past, but then a new clue came forth that he had never seen before. The man, who was stabbing Kim with the knife, was left-handed, and he was a white man. He saw the Flagg's patch again, and this time he saw another patch over the guy's pocket. It said, "Skip." Then something he had never seen before. A bright flash as the man had taken a picture of Kim nude. Barry woke up, sitting upright in bed and hugging his knees to his chest. *Why, after all of these years, was this coming out?* Something eerie was happening. Maybe the trance he had been put in back in Fairbanks was still working, still releasing tiny bits of information, piece by piece. If only it could, or would, tell him who it was that killed Kim. He looked at the clock. He had only been in bed about an hour.

Torch was on his way back to Minneapolis empty-handed, but with a whole new perspective on Barry Winston. He was going to have a conversation with Ray before he worked on this case any farther. The plane rose high in the sky over Fairbanks, and banked to the south. Below him were mountains as far as the eye could see, and several rivers snaking their way between them. It was all grey and white in the Yukon—traditional winter colors.

Detective Kemper was at the guest registration at the Travelers Inn, waiting his turn to talk to Dean Simpson, the night clerk who had checked Darien Frisco in the other night. Right now, he was busy checking in a young couple who looked like, unless they got in a room quick, they were going to copulate right there in the lobby. He gave them their room key cards and then turned, smiling, at Clarence. "How can I help you?" he asked.

The detective flipped his badge open, and then slid the registration card across the counter with Darien Frisco's name on it. "This man checked in here the other night, only to turn up dead the next morning. Ring a bell?"

"No, sir...I check in a lot of people, detective."

Next came a picture of Darien, taken at the morgue. "How about now?"

"No, sir. I don't remember renting a room to that man. What's the matter with him? He looks awful."

"Well, that's because he's dead. Are there security cameras here?"

"Just the exits and the hallways."

"That exit?" The detective indicated the front entrance.

"No, we're right here, so we can watch that one."

"I need the exit tapes for the last week."

"Can I ask why, detective?"

"Yeah, we're looking for a murder suspect."

The clerk furrowed his wide brow as he asked, "That death wasn't an overdose?"

"Most likely not. Do you care if I look around."

"No, help yourself." He motioned to the hallway that led to the guest rooms.

Detective Kemper walked down the carpeted hallway to the elevators. This had happened on the third floor, so whoever did this probably used those elevators. Then he noticed the exit door right beside the lifts. He went over and was going to push the panic bar to see what was outside, but noticed the warning in bold letters, **Warning—bells will ring.** Then he saw the cut wires going to the battery box.

With the tapes from the security system in hand, the detective made his way back to headquarters. Back at his desk there was a note to call the lab as soon as possible.

"Turner, Lab," the voice said. Kemper was still standing in front of his desk with his coat on.

"Yeah, Turner. Detective Kemper, what you got?"

"Hey, man. We ran those prints on that room card. One isn't a match, but the other one is a friend of yours."

"Who's that?" he said.

"Skip Henderson."

Back at the police station receptionist desk, the detective told the attendant, "Going back to the Travelers Inn."

Back at the hotel, he approached the desk once more. This time it was just he and the clerk. "Simpson…right?"

"That's right, detective. What do you need now?"

"Just want you to look at a picture." Clarence slid five mugs shots on the same paper across the counter. "Anyone look familiar?" he asked.

Simpson pulled his glasses down off his forehead and looked at the pictures. Then he put his finger on the picture of Skip Henderson.

"That's the man who rented the room, detective. Oh! Wow…that's not the dead man, is it?"

"Thanks, Simpson. You've been a great help. Tell your maintenance people the alarm is broken on the exit door at the end of the hall. Someone cut the wires." He turned and walked out.

Torch was back in Minneapolis. His flight had touched down in a snowstorm the night before. He and Charlie had talked into the wee hours of the morning. She had hinted at making love when they went to bed, but by the time they got around to it, they were both too tired, so she said, "Can I have a rain check?"

Torch didn't answer, so she turned on the lamp and looked at his face. He was sleeping.

The following morning, Torch was walking up the steps to City Hall with a manila folder in his hand. He had a nine o'clock meeting with Ray.

Ray was staring out the office window, watching a few leftover snowflakes coming down from the snow last night, when Torch got to the office. The streets were slushy and pedestrians were walking like penguins on the treacherous footing, something most Minnesotans learned to master early in life. He turned and looked at Torch as he came into the room.

"Hell, I expected you to have frostbite or something," he mused.

"Nope, it's colder here than there, I think."

"So, no prisoner brought back, I take it."

"Far as I know, he's already back here in the city, Ray."

"Why? How?" Ray asked.

"Well, it's a long story. How about we go to Whitey's for coffee, and I'll fill you in."

The café was almost deserted as the breakfast crowd was gone, and it was too early for lunch. A sign said, **Seat yourself** and another said, **Today's special -meatloaf sandwich for five bucks.**

"There's a damn crime happening right here," Ray said. "Poisoning people with that horsemeat. These people learn how to cook anything but meatloaf, or what they call meatloaf?"

"Watch your tongue," Torch said. "That's a signature sandwich. You always were a fussy basterd. Shame on your mother for spoiling the shit out of you."

"Up yours," said Ray.

Torch didn't know how to start with what he had to say, so he just said it. "Ray, Barry is most likely innocent. I know a lot of people always thought he was, but not me, and now I'm convinced he was."

"Well, what brought this on?" Ray asked.

Torch went through the whole nine yards. He talked about the meeting with Audrey, the priest and the doctor. Explained that Barry was in cancer treatment, and most likely wouldn't live that long. How he had hid out in the wilderness for four years, and just recently came out of hiding.

The waitress was back to refill their cups. "Anything to eat, boys?"

"Not for me," Torch said, "But Ray here could use a meatloaf sandwich to go."

"Jeeze, Torch, you want me to puke right here on the table?" he said.

Torch laughed. "Bring us both a Danish," he said.

"So what do you want to do?" Ray asked. "The man has a murder rap against him. We can't just make that go away."

"No, but we can help him find Skip."

"Then what? Vigilante justice? Give him a gun and watch him shoot the worthless bastard?"

"Well, I hope not, but let's see if we can get him to trust us. I think he knows more answers than we do when it comes to Skip."

"So how?" Ray was listening intently.

"Well, he's got some evidence we never had, something the courts wouldn't accept as evidence back then, but they might now. I went through those files again, Ray, and I have to admit...we were damn lucky to get a conviction on what we presented as evidence back then."

"Can you be more specific?" Ray asked.

"I could, but I think it would be better if Barry told it to you. Look, he came back here to find Skip, so maybe we can help him there. Skip has been thumbing his nose at us for a long time. He shouldn't be that hard to find."

132

Ray shrugged his shoulders, "It's your baby, Torch. Go for it, but I have no idea where Skip is."

"I still have some snitches I used to work with. Let me ask around." Torch pushed the tab across the table at Ray.

"Hey, you cheap bastard, coming here was your idea." Ray picked it up, chuckling.

Back at the office, Torch asked Ray to put out a search for Skip and let him know if, or when, he found him.

Soon after Torch left, Ray took a call from a detective in Charleston, South Carolina. His name was Kemper, and he wanted someone to keep a lookout for Skip Henderson."'

"We are looking for him, too. What did he do now?" Ray asked.

"Murder one," Kemper said, "and we have a lot of proof."

"When did this happen?" Ray asked.

"Day before yesterday."

"You think he's flying back here?"

"Well, we checked the airport and no one by his name flew out, but he's got more aliases than Mickey Rooney's got wives."

"Thanks for the heads up," Ray said. "We'll be in touch."

He grabbed his hat and coat and stopping at the receptionist desk said, "Jenny, I'm on my way to the airport. Back in a couple of hours. I have a hunch to play out."

CHAPTER TWENTY-ONE

Barry had taken a cab over to the offices of Twin City Parcel Services. It wasn't that far from where he was staying, and he had planned on walking it, but he wasn't feeling real good today. *Must have been something I ate,* he thought. He had thrown up during the night, but his stomach felt better now. The doctors in Fairbanks had given him a prescription for some stomach pills, and maybe he would get it filled. He'd had problems with his stomach ever since the chemo.

After the cab dropped him off, he walked up the sidewalk to the vine-covered red brick building, now denuded by winter. Inside, the receptionist desk was the first thing he came to. A very pretty black lady asked if she could direct him. She was older, maybe in her late forties, but the years had been kind to her and she was trim and fit. The nameplate on her desk said **Doris Malone - Receptionist**. "I'm looking for the personnel manager," Barry said.

"She is out until tomorrow. Is there something I can help you with?"

"Ah. Well, maybe. I'm trying to find the address of a former, or maybe a present employee of this company. I'm not sure what his status is."

"That kind of information would have to come from the personnel manager, if we have it. I say if, because…was this from a long time ago or fairly recent?"

Barry cleared his throat. "Well, it was from almost twenty years ago when the firm was called Flagg's, but like I said, I don't know how long he worked here or if he still does."

Doris had her pen poised over a yellow-lined tablet. "Why don't you give me the employee's name, and when she gets back maybe she can help you. I don't know for sure."

Barry hesitated, "I only have a first name."

"Wow, that might be hard, but give it to me, anyway."

"Skip," said Barry.

Doris's faced turned ashen. "Can I ask you what this is about?"

Barry hesitated again. He had come too far to stop now. "I think he was the man who killed my wife."

Doris said, "Excuse me," and she went into the office behind her to compose herself, leaving Barry standing at the counter. *What was she going to do? She couldn't release any information from the company but she could tell him a lot about Skip. Damn it, she always knew Skip was the one.* She wiped her eyes before she came back out.

"What is your name?" she asked, "and where can I get ahold of you, later today?"

"My name is Barry Winston, and I'm staying at this phone number." He wrote it down on the corner of her pad of yellow paper, and tore it off, handing it to her.

Doris's hands were shaking, "I'll call you," she said. "I promise you, I'll call you."

"Thanks," Barry said. "Hey, by the way, does the name Cheryl Cousins ring a bell with you? He had no idea why he had asked her that. There were a million people in this city, and she couldn't possible know her. *My God, he was grasping at straws here.* Barry couldn't help feeling he had hit a nerve with her when he said, "Skip," but now she looked doubly troubled when he mentioned Cheryl. She sure had changed in a hurry, and not for the good.

"I'll call you," she said, without answering his question. Now her lips were trembling, too, and she quickly put her hand up there to hide her concern, as other people in the office were noticing something wasn't right.

He was feeling better, so he decided to walk back. Besides, it was a nice afternoon. He had hit a nerve with Doris. *She knew more than she was willing to say right now.* He had to see her again.

Doris sat in the bathroom stall, crying softly. *Yes, she knew Cheryl, and so did Skip. They had delivered hundreds of packages there before she was promoted to the office. She also knew a woman named Kim Winston once. She worked with Cheryl.*

She reached over and took some tissue of the paper roll and wiped her eyes and blew her nose in it. *She would call Barry Winston, but not before she called Torch Brennan.*

Torch, now at home and reading the paper, looked at his ringing phone, eyeing it suspiciously. *Who could this be?* "Brennan," he answered.

"Mr. Brennan, this is Doris Malone. Do you remember me? Can I talk with you again?"

"Certainly I remember you. Is something wrong? Do you want me to come out to your place?"

"Yes. It's in regard to Skip Henderson."

"Did he try to contact you?"

"No, but someone else did, someone who is also looking for him."

"I'll be right there," he said.

He grabbed his address book and his car keys, and met Charlie coming in the door, as he was going out. "Back soon, honey."

"Torch, where you going? It's five thirty. Are you going to be here for supper?" Charlie had an exasperated look on her face. Her arms were full of bags of groceries.

"Not sure, dear, and I'm in a hurry. I'll call you as soon as I know more." He blew her a kiss, and was down the driveway and into his car. It was rush hour and the traffic was going to suck.

Barry was feeling punk again and he was lying down when Father Murphy came to the door and knocked lightly. "Barry, are you awake?" he said, peering around the door.

"Ah, yes, Father. I seem to have the flu or something. What's going on?"

"There is a Doris Malone on the line for you. You can take the call in my study, if you want."

Ray was in the security office at the airport, talking with the Chief of Security. "What I want to know, my friend, is if a certain person arrived on a Delta flight from Charleston, either yesterday, or the day before?"

"Well, we have the manifests from the flight—or at least I can get them. We also have the pictures that the security cameras take of people debarking. Is that enough?"

"I don't know...it might be. If it isn't, I might need to talk to the attendants who worked the flights."

"That could be tougher. Most of them aren't based right here, so they could be anywhere in the system right now."

"Let's look at the pictures first." Ray said.

The chief took him down to an office in the lower level. He talked with a man there who seemed to be amused by the whole thing, or at least by something. Finally, between his fits of amusement, he said, "Give me a few minutes." The two men sat down and talked about business and security at the airport, and how it had changed over the years. Ray had started out in police work at the airport.

A few minutes later, the joker was back and said, "Follow me."

They went down a narrow corridor to a small room with a large TV screen and several folding chairs. "These can take a while," the man said. "They like to take their own time leaving. The first film is from yesterday, and the other is from the day before. Just shut off the light when you're done. The controls for the projector are right there on the wall."

"Thanks," Ray said.

He was the third person off on the second film. Ray wasn't sure but after he reran it the second time he was certain. He'd only met Skip a couple of times, but it was a face you didn't forget.

"That's him?" the Chief said.

"I think so. Can I see the manifest?"

The chief handed over the copy, and Ray scanned through it. "Not on there," he said, "but that doesn't surprise me. He's got a lot of names. Thanks. I'll let myself out."

"Barry, this is Doris. I have only a few minutes, but I need to tell you something." Barry was sitting at Father Murphy's desk in a reclining leather chair, but he wasn't relaxing, he was holding his forehead trying to see if he had a fever.

"Barry, I don't know if I can help you right now, but I will know more tomorrow after I talk to someone else, who I think, is trying to reach the same man you are. I'll call you back tomorrow evening, okay?"

Torch had only been at Doris's house once before, and it had been at the start of winter. He remembered all too well what an emotional day it had been. In spite of only being here that one time, he drove right up to the door. It was warmer than usual today, for late winter, and the streets were slushy and filled with ridges and ruts. The tires were sending up torrents of that icy sludge against the floorboards of the car, and it made steering difficult.

He pushed the doorbell and it opened immediately, as if she had been waiting for him right there behind the door. Torch stepped in and Doris looked around him, and outside, seemingly making sure he was alone. She was dressed in white sweat pants and a loose fitting top. Her hair looked as if she had just run her fingers through it, instead of a comb. "Hi, Mr. Brennan," she said. "Thank you for coming out." She took his coat and hat and laid it across the back of an over stuffed chair. "Let's go into the kitchen. I made some coffee."

"Mr. Brennan…"

"Torch," he interjected, "Call me Torch."

"The last time you were here, Torch, you were looking for Skip Henderson. Did you ever find him?"

"Well, we were looking for more than Skip. If you recall, we were looking for the evidence we needed to arrest him and prosecute him. We pretty much knew where he was, we just couldn't arrest him for anything because he did a good job of putting the fear of God in everyone, and no one would talk."

"But the one crime—and I take it he has done many—which you were trying to arrest him for, was the murder of Kim Winston, were you not?" Doris was pouring coffee as she spoke, and had set a plate of cookies on the table.

"Doris, a man has already been convicted of murdering Kim Winston." He stopped to dip his cookie in his coffee." There was, at the time, some evidence that Skip was involved, and the man who was convicted may not have been."

"Was that man Kim's husband?"

"Yes, what do you know about him?"

"First of all, are you trying to arrest him?"

"At the time I talked to you before, I was. I'm not sure about it anymore, though."

"What would you do if you caught him?"

"Maybe help him prove his innocence. Why all this interest in Barry Winston, Doris?"

"Because I know where he is."

Torch was quiet and thinking. Doris was trying to cut a deal with him and he knew it. "If you will arrange a meeting with him, I promise not to arrest him."

"You promise no one will arrest him?"

"I can't promise that, but I will tell you this. If he is arrested, I will have had nothing to do with it."

"Can you come here tomorrow?"

"Yes."

"I will try and arrange it if I can. I'll call you tonight. More coffee?"

Torch was going to tell Ray what he had found out, but now he realized he couldn't. He better go home and keep his mouth shut. "No, but thank you," he said.

For the first time since he arrived in the city, Barry called Audrey. The phone rang several times, but just before it went to the machine, it was picked up and a sleepy voice said, "Hi."

"Audrey, it's me."

"Oh my God, Barry," she said, clearing her throat. "I was waiting for you to call. I worked the night shift last night, so I was sleeping. Are you okay?"

"Yes, I'm fine. Scared that I'm going to get caught, but fine."

"You sound funny. Your voice sounds weak."

"Well, I was sick yesterday but I'm better now. I think I had the flu or something."

"You don't sound better."

"You can tell that from three thousand miles away?"

"Barry, I'm a nurse, and I know you. Yes, I can tell that. How goes the search?"

"Audrey, I had another dream. I know who the man is now. Tomorrow I'm meeting with a woman who might be able to help me. I think she knew him."

"Have you seen a doctor about your treatments yet? You were supposed to do that right away, Barry." Suddenly, she seemed disinterested in his search.

"Maybe tomorrow," he said.

"Barry, I love you. Please take care of yourself. You've got the number for the doctor, call him."

"I have to go," he said. "I love you too, Audrey." He hung up the phone. Maybe he should go see that doctor. He did have a fever and it wasn't going away.

CHAPTER TWENTY-TWO

Torch had a message from Ray when he got home. "Call me," it said. It was after five when he called, and Ray had gone home for the day. The receptionist gave him Ray's cell number so he called him on that.

"Ray...Torch. What did you want? I'm tired and I'm staying home tonight with my wife, just in case you have something exciting for me to do..."

"Torch, I just wanted to tell you that I got word that Skip was back in Charleston where he murdered some druggie. They have him dead to rights. But get this, he flew back here and today I saw his picture on an airline security camera. So most likely, he's in town. All we have to do is find him. What's new in your little world?"

Torch was quiet for a second. He knew that tomorrow he was going to meet up with the man he had been hunting, for almost twenty years, and he had no intention of doing anything but to help this man find justice and closure for the killing of his wife. He was not so sure that he and Ray were on the same page with this, so he didn't mention it. "Got some leads I'm working on, but basically, not much. Taking it one day at a time."

"Well, keep in touch. Keep me up on what you find out."

"Will do," Torch said.

Charlie walked into the room and sat on his lap. He was sitting on a kitchen chair with the phone still in his hand. "You always want to be on top," he said, kissing her behind her ear.

"Oh, shut up, Torch, and listen. I have tickets to the Orpheum tonight."

"For what?" Torch asked.

"Phantom of the Opera."

"Be still my beating heart," Torch answered.

"Yeah, well, if you ever want to see me on top of you again, you will go shower and put some decent clothes on. The show starts at eight, and you still have to wine and dine me."

It would be fun to go have a night out with his beloved. All this cop stuff was driving him nuts, but he couldn't help but feel apprehensive about meeting Barry Winston tomorrow.

Barry was in the office of Dr. Sheldon Perry, at University hospital, close to downtown Minneapolis. He had passed out this afternoon, and when he called the doctor, from the number his oncologist in Fairbanks had given him, they had told him to come right over. Regular hours were over, but Dr. Sheldon would stay late to see him.

He was sitting on the examination table in his underwear. "Does this hurt when I press here?" he was pushing in on the right side of Barry's abdomen.

Barry winced. "Yes," he said, barely audible.

"Barry, I want you to go over to the main hospital so we can run some tests. I'm not going to be able to diagnose you here, but my gut feeling says your liver is acting up again. The x-rays you had done last month in Fairbanks show some form of abnormality there yet, but I'm not sure what it is."

Barry looked dejected. *Was his cancer back? Was this disease going to stop him from clearing his name when he'd come this far?*

"Can it wait until the day after tomorrow?"

"I suppose, but what's so important?" the doctor looked annoyed. He had stayed late to see this man, and now he was not being cooperative.

"If I told you the whole story we would be here a long time Doc. Believe me, it's important, and I have to do it tomorrow. It's all set up."

"Suit yourself. I'll set up your test for Thursday. Be there. In the meantime, I'm going to have my nurse give you an IV with some antibiotics in it. Your fever is high and your white blood cells are way out of line. Something's going on."

The doctor left and the nurse came in with a bag of solution. "Make a fist," she said, as she pressed down on the vein in his arm, and anchoring it, she inserted the needle that was attached to the drip line of the IV bag. "You need to just relax for the next half hour and let this finish dripping. I'll be in the next room. Holler for me when the bag is empty."

As Barry lay there, watching the solution dripping into his arm, he knew something was drastically wrong with his body. He didn't have a fear of dying anymore, he just had a fear of dying guilty, and he needed his day in court.

An hour later, he walked out into early evening, across the river from downtown Minneapolis. The lights of the city seemed to bring it new life at night and he loved the city. He didn't want to live there, but he still loved it. For some reason, he was very apprehensive right now. Barry just wanted to get this thing resolved and head back to Fairbanks; to the woman he knew he loved. He went into a 'back to the fifties' restaurant, a block from Dinky Town, and sat down. He could use a good hamburger and chocolate malt.

Skip was back on the north side, and just as the cops had their snitches, he had his. He knew there was an all-points bulletin out for his arrest, and he knew it was for the murder of Darien. But Skip had a lot of ties to the north side underworld, and for the time being, they could keep him safe.

Doris stood looking out over her back yard. In the background, the coffee maker was spitting out coffee into a glass carafe. On the table was a fresh jellyroll she had made this morning. Calling in sick to work this morning, and lying to them about being sick, hadn't been easy. She took pride in being an honest person, but she was tired of living in fear, and now this was her chance to do a very good deed— to help this poor man, who had lived in exile all of these years, find justice.

There was a knock on the door, and she looked up at the clock. It was 10 a.m. She went to the door and looked out the sidelight window. It was a man she didn't know, and she could only assume it was Barry Winston.

"Barry?" she said.

"Hi," he said, weakly.

"Barry, I'm so glad to meet you. My name is Doris Malone, and I might have gotten off on the wrong foot the last time I talked to you. I think the person you are looking for is someone I knew very well,

and that startled me at the time. Come on in, and we can talk more."
She showed him the way to the kitchen, and offered him a chair. "I
have some coffee that will be done in minute," she said.

"Thanks," Barry said.

She sat down across the table from him. "Barry, before we talk,
I want you to know that, in a few minutes, another man is coming
in to join us. I don't want you to get alarmed, but he is a former
Minneapolis Police Detective. He wants you to know, that despite
all of the years they spent looking for you, he doesn't want to detain
you. He knows you are innocent and he wants to help you, but you
have to trust him."

"Is his name Brennan?" Barry asked.

"Yes."

Barry started to push his chair back, as if he was trying to get up,
but Doris reached across the table and said, "Barry, please trust us."

A part of him wanted to get up and run out the door, but something
in her eyes told him that she was his only chance, and he had no
choice but to trust her. Besides, he was getting sick again, and he
needed to settle down. Last night had been a bad night. He was up
most of the night, throwing up that hamburger, fries and malt that
had tasted so good last night. It was as if everything just turned to
fire in his belly.

Just then, there was a knock at the door. Doris went over and
opened the door to let Torch in. Barry could hear them talking softly
by the door for a couple of minutes, and then the door closed and
Torch was standing in the kitchen doorway, looking at Barry. He
couldn't believe his eyes. This was the defiant man he had testified
against at the trial so many years ago, and now he was slumped in
this wooden chair, looking gaunt, jaundiced and defeated. Barry tried
to stand, but Torch said, "No, please sit," and sat down beside him.
"You look terrible, Barry, are you sick?"

Barry nodded his head. "I have cancer," he said. "I was in
remission, but I think it's back. That's all the more reason I need to
find Kim's killer. I can't die in peace until he's caught."

Doris was holding a paper towel to her face and crying softly into
it, but saying nothing.

"Barry, I want you to get medical attention as soon as you can.
Tell me your side of the story one more time."

For the next half hour, Barry talked. He talked about the night of the killing; he talked about the trial and his run from justice. Then he talked about the visions he had over the years, and his time in hypnosis. He described Skip Henderson completely. He even talked about the vision he had of the man taking a photograph of Kim's dead body. A man he didn't know, and had never met in real life, but a man Torch knew well and Doris knew even better.

Everything was falling into place for Torch. "Barry, we have a warrant out for his arrest right now. Last we knew, he was here in Minneapolis. I promise you every cop in the city is looking for him, and I promise you, we will catch him."

Sweat was pouring off Barry's forehead. Torch reached over and took his hand and then, looking down at Barry's bent-over body, he said, "Let's get you to a doctor." He walked Barry to his car and then said, "Just a minute, I have to say goodbye to Doris." He walked back up to the front door where she was standing. "Thanks for your help, Doris," he said. "I'll be in touch." He turned his head and looked at Barry, now sitting in the car. "We'll take good care of him." He got in his car, and soon they were turning onto I-94, heading for downtown and University Hospital. Once they arrived at the hospital, he stayed with Barry until he was checked in, and then told him, "Call me if you need anything. Right now, I have a murderer to catch."

CHAPTER TWENTY-THREE

When Barry woke up, he hardly remembered being in E.R. and subsequently, being admitted to the hospital. He had IVs in both arms and, in his nose, an oxygen tube, which made little hissing noises each time he breathed. He could see a nurse in the corridor but there was no one else in the room. Feeling along the rail on the side of the bed, he found the remote and pushed the button. The nurse he could see out in the corridor, turned around and came in the open door.

"Yes, Mr. Winston?" she said.

"Where are my clothes?" he asked. "I can't stay here. Not yet."

"Please lay back down and I'll try to get your doctor."

Realizing, that even if he could find his clothes, he didn't have the strength to get in them, he settled back down onto the pillow.

Suddenly, he was aware of a young man in blue hospital scrubs standing over his bed, holding a chart. The nurse he had talked to was standing beside him.

"Mr. Winston. I'm Dr. Eli. I don't have your entire test results back yet, but I have enough to be able to tell you, you are a very sick man. Were you aware you have cancer?"

"Yes. My records are up in Fairbanks," he said.

"Alaska?" the doctor asked.

Barry nodded his head.

"Well, at this stage of the game, I'm not sure if we need them or not. Would you like me to talk to your doctor up there?"

Barry said, "How long do I have?"

"If we can stop the pneumonia, maybe a few weeks. I'm not an oncologist but you will be seeing one, and he'll have a better idea. You are very sick, my friend, and you have a lot of infection to fight off, and not much left to fight it with."

"Would you call someone else in Alaska for me?"

"Sure. Just give me a name and number."

"Doc, please call the Fairbanks City Hospital. Ask for Audrey Snyder. She's a nurse on the fourth floor. If she's not working, leave a message to have her call me here."

"Okay, will do. Who's this Skip you kept mumbling about when you first came in? Do you need us to call him?"

"No, I think I know where he is. I'll take care of it." Just then, Torch walked in.

"How you doing, buddy," Torch said.

"Better than yesterday," said Barry, "but the news isn't good. Sit down and I'll tell you about it."

"They told me in Fairbanks about your cancer. Is that the problem now?"

Barry nodded his head. "I wanted so badly to see justice before I died." His eyes were welling with tears, and he talked between gasps of breath.

"Well, hang onto that dream, my friend. I talked with my boss today, and they have every available cop looking for this guy. He's not going to get far. Barry, I have something I want to say, and it's not easy for me, but it needs to be said. Sometimes in police work, we get tunnel vision. Sometimes, all of the evidence points at the wrong people and we get lazy, and don't really pursue the case. Our justice system has so many impediments built into it that the guilty people have learned to use to their advantage. There are also attorneys that will go to the ends of the earth to represent these people. Far more guilty people go free, than innocent people like you get charged. But that's not an excuse to not get it right. It's just a reason."

"I called Audrey and she's coming down to see you. Your doctor asked me to, when I called to see how you were doing. He was having trouble getting ahold of her, and I had her home number."

Barry had been listening all along, but when Torch said Audrey's name, he perked up. "When? How?" he asked.

"She's flying down today, and I'm picking her up at the airport."

Barry smiled, but then he had a coughing spell and Torch called for a nurse. When she came in, she listened to his chest, and then she gave him a shot to settle him down. "He needs to rest," she said.

"Yes. I was just leaving," Torch answered.

She sat looking out the small oval window of the aircraft, her hanky balled up in her hand. Beneath the plane were the white-capped mountains of Southern Alaska. Barry's doctor, at the Fairbanks hospital, had talked with the oncologist at the Minneapolis hospital. They had said he wasn't doing well and they felt it wouldn't be long.

She thought back to when she had first met this strange man. Beneath that quiet demeanor he showed her, she always felt there was something that was tearing him apart, and now she knew.

Sarah was with her grandmother for a few days. Although she had no time for her former husband, she still loved the old woman, and so did Sarah. She looked out the window again. The mountains had given way to the prairies of Western Canada, dotted with lakes and rivers, and something that was rare in Alaska—towns.

Audrey turned and smiled at Father Kevin, who was sitting beside her, and he reached over and touched her arm. He, like Barry, had a mission, too. Barry couldn't die without clearing his name and saving his reputation, and Father Kevin wasn't going to let him die without also saving his soul.

At four thirty that afternoon, while Torch was bringing Audrey and Father Kevin to the hospital, his cell phone rang.

"Torch, this is Ray. Where are you?"

"I'm on my way back from the airport."

"Well, we have Skip cornered in an apartment on North Freemont. He says he's not coming out alive. Swat team is in place, trying to talk him out of it."

"Let me drop off some people, and then I'll be up. Where are you?"

"On my way down there. It's the twenty nine hundred block."

"Torch smiled at Audrey, "Sorry about that, just a little business."

Father Kevin spoke up from the back seat, "It never ends does it, Detective."

"This time it's going to end, Father. This time it's going to." He pulled up to the main entrance of the hospital. "He's in room four fourteen. I have some business to take care of and then I'll be back to pick you up."

They made their way up to Barry's room. He was on oxygen, but alert, when they walked into the room. Audrey sat on the edge of the bed, running her hands through his hair, and crying softly. Barry seemed to know they were there, but he wasn't talking.

Father Kevin opened his bag and brought out the things he would need for giving Barry the last rites. Audrey held his hands as the young priest performed the sacred ritual so essential to all Catholics. When he was finished, and all of the prayers were over, he said to Barry, "You're good to go, my friend." Then he pulled a chair up to the edge of the bed across from Audrey, and each of them took a hand. Nighttime was settling over the city, and down below you could see and hear the sounds of traffic; but in the room, all was quiet save for the hissing of the breathing machine.

When Torch pulled up to the scene, the Swat team was packing up. Ray spotted him and came down to talk to him, as he stood on the sidewalk in front of the house. "It's all over, Torch. He did himself in."

"That's good," Torch said. "No sense making some cop responsible for ending his measly life. It's a coward's way out but it's the best way for us. Maybe he finally did something right. Can I see?"

They walked upstairs into the upper floor of a duplex, and through a sparsely furnished living room, into a bedroom. He lay sprawled on the bed, the gun still in his hand. A large red spot was in the white tee top he had been wearing. A hole was right over his heart.

"Check his I.D," Torch said. Ray rolled him partway over and took out his wallet. His wallet was thick with fake ID cards, and Ray pulled out half a dozen of them.

"Take your pick," he said. Then, in a pocket under the cards, he pulled out a stack of pictures and started looking through them. The last picture was barely in one piece, but it was clearly a nude woman who had just been murdered, and lying beside her was the arm and left leg of a man who didn't fit into the picture. Torch said, "It's Kim." Barry told me...aw, never mind. I have the file at home. I'll put this in there, Ray, and bring the whole file in to you on Monday."

"What's Monday?" Ray said.

"My last day at work, Ray." Torch turned and walked out. Outside the door, he reached for his cigarettes and lit one. Torch inhaled deeply, and looked around the scene. Then he fished in his pocket and took out that weathered photograph of Kim. He lit his lighter once more, and set the picture on fire. He held it until he almost burnt his fingers, and then dropped it in the gutter, along with his pack of cigarettes.

Audrey and the priest were still sitting in the room when Torch got back.

"Did you catch the guy?" Father Kevin asked.

"Yes, he's dead. When did Barry die?"

"About five minutes ago."

"I wished he could have lived to have known that." Audrey said.

"I'm betting he knew about it," Torch said. He didn't explain himself. Something told him the other two knew all too well what he was talking about. Torch sat down on the edge of the bed, and took Barry's lifeless hand in his. Audrey had been sitting there, but now she was crying softly in a chair in the corner of the room, with Father Kevin trying to console her.

"You were right, my friend," Torch said to Barry. "You were right, and for so long I was wrong, but justice has been served at last, and for that I will be eternally grateful." He paused to wipe a tear from his face. Then he kissed Barry on the forehead.

Standing up, he said to Father Kevin and Audrey, "Thanks to both of you for being his friend when he needed one so badly. I want you to know there was a small reward for Skip's capture, and Barry's clues kind of cracked the case for us. I'll see his estate gets the money. It will be enough to bury him next to Kim. I have already made the arrangements, if that's all right, and what's left over, Father, I will send up to you. Maybe you can buy something nice for the church."

"Thank you," the priest said. "May he rest in peace."

"Audrey," Torch went on, "he loved you. He told me so. I hope you know that it was only with your help that he was able to accomplish his wish to clear his name." She nodded her head and then, walking over to the bed, she bent down and kissed Barry softly. Father Kevin took her hand and the three of them walked out of the room together.

EPILOGUE

Three weeks later, Audrey got a box from Torch with a note attached, that simply said, "Barry wanted you to have this." She sat down at the kitchen table and unwrapped the box. Inside was just an envelope in Barry's handwriting, and a small leather pouch. Carefully, she opened the envelope and took out the note. It was written on hospital stationary.

Dear Audrey.

I wanted so badly for us to live the rest of our lives together. Had I not met you I would have died a very lonely and supposedly guilty man. There is something in a man's make up called pride, and although mine was bruised and busted, you helped me find it. I did love you, my friend, so much, and it felt so right. I know now, here in this hospital bed, that I won't live much longer, but that's all right, too, because I know that where I am going, you will be there someday also. Thank Father for me, and Dr. Bob, and all the good people of Fairbanks who believed in me. I'll see you on the other side.
Barry

She cried softly for a while, and then wiped her eyes on the corner of the tablecloth. It was then she saw the leather pouch she had set off to the side, and she picked it up and unzipped it. It was full of wild rice, and down in the bottom was the dehydrated body of a little mouse, perfectly preserved.

Mike Holst

CPSIA information can be obtained at www.ICGtesting.com
Printed in the USA
BVOW07s1946260614

357504BV00001B/10/P

9 781491 737835